DEADLY WILDERNESS SHOWDOWN

LISA WEAVER

LOVE INSPIRED SUSPENSE
INSPIRATIONAL ROMANCE

Recycling programs for this product may not exist in your area.

ISBN-13: 978-1-335-95786-3

Deadly Wilderness Showdown

For questions and comments about the quality of this book, please contact us at CustomerService@Harlequin.com.

Love Inspired
22 Adelaide St. West, 41st Floor
Toronto, Ontario M5H 4E3, Canada
www.LoveInspired.com

HarperCollins Publishers
Macken House, 39/40 Mayor Street Upper,
Dublin 1, D01 C9W8, Ireland
www.HarperCollins.com

Printed in Lithuania

1 2 3 4 5 6 7 8 9 10 LIT 28 27 26 25

The Jeep gained momentum and drew up behind them.

Stomping on the gas pedal again, Ethan sent his truck racing forward. The Jeep driver copied the maneuver. It was only a matter of time before the man pursuing them made his move.

Ethan's brow furrowed. "Roll your window down and have your gun ready in case things go south," he instructed Abbie.

Seeing the driver lining up to strike, he swung the wheel sharply. Swerving back and forth as far as the narrow road would allow, he heard the whine of the Jeep's engine. The vehicle was close. Too close.

Ethan's hands contracted on the wheel. "Brace yourself," he warned Abbie.

The jolt came hard and fast, accompanied by the screeching crunch of metal abrading metal. It took all of his skill to keep the truck from veering into the cliffside. Accelerating again, he managed to put space between them and the Jeep. His heart hammered in his chest as he realized it wasn't going to be enough.

He had two options, neither of them good.

Lisa Weaver lives in Maine with her husband and one very spoiled Maine coon cat. When she's not spinning pulse-pounding tales, she enjoys hiking, biking, getting her hands dirty in her flower gardens, spending time in nature and baking decadent treats inspired by her fascination with baking competition shows (and chocolate).

Books by Lisa Weaver

Love Inspired Suspense

Deadly Wilderness Showdown

Visit the Author Profile page at LoveInspired.com.

The Lord is my light and my salvation;
whom shall I fear? the Lord is the strength of my life;
of whom shall I be afraid?
—*Psalms* 27:1

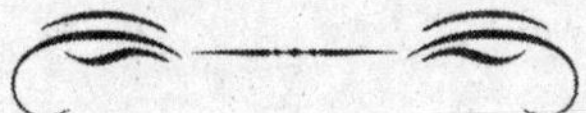

This book is dedicated to my husband, Duane,
the inspiration for all my fictional heroes.

ONE

Abbie Renforth had witnessed more than her share of psyche-scarring moments in her former career as a photojournalist for an international news agency. She'd captured far too many heart-wrenching images in the aftermath of earthquakes, floods, wildfires and senseless crimes than she cared to remember. Some things, once seen, could never be unseen.

She'd experienced the worst the world had to offer—and not only in her professional life. Now, amid the wild and rugged beauty of Maine, where she'd retreated after losing her job and very nearly her life, she was experiencing the best.

Recalling how close she'd come to missing out on the chance to spend three months in this idyllic expanse of backcountry courtesy of a visiting artist program, she was grateful she'd overcome her hesitation. Fear had nearly kept her from saying yes when she'd first been offered the opportunity to take part in this once-in-a-lifetime experience. Since she'd been attacked, her formerly borderless comfort zone had shrunk to an anxiety-restricted microcosm. Nearly dying at the hands of a demented serial killer had a way of doing that to a person.

Fortunately, her desire to embrace the opportunity to stretch her creative wings in the solitude of the backcountry had outweighed her insecurities. She was glad she'd pushed past her trepidation, because the reservations she'd harbored about accepting the offer to take part in the program so soon after the horrific ordeal she'd survived had been quashed the moment she'd arrived.

From the bold little chickadee who'd perched on an evergreen branch beside her while she was eating lunch, his astute black eyes on the lookout for crumbs, to the red squirrel who'd scolded her for having the audacity to set foot on his turf, to the behemoth of a moose standing hip-deep in a tranquil lake contentedly feasting on water lilies—there couldn't be a more ideal pool of subjects for her nature photos than the vast array of creatures great and small who called this paradise home.

She was only a week into the adventure of launching her new career as a freelance wildlife photographer, but her time here had already injected her with a renewed sense of purpose and some much-needed hope.

The instant she'd stepped over the threshold of the sumptuously appointed haven of a cabin that would be her home from June through August, peace had settled around her. Her first night here, tucked into a ginormous bed that would have taken up half her studio apartment back in New York, she'd been lulled to sleep by the call of loons and the cool, pine-scented breeze wafting in the windows.

To her amazement, she hadn't been yanked from slumber a single time by one of the heart-stopping, terrifying nightmares that had hijacked her dreams the past four months. It was the first peaceful night she'd experienced since the Spitting Image Slayer had tried to make her his next victim.

By God's mercy, she'd survived the demented serial killer's savage attempt to end her life. The ordeal had changed her, though. She'd gone from intrepidly exposing injustices to being scared of her own shadow—her former nerves of steel reduced to quivering jelly. The faintest unexpected noise, or the merest glimpse of something out of the ordinary, was all it took to trigger memories of the attack and yank her back into the pit of terror she'd clawed her way out of.

She was trying hard to put the horror of that unimaginable night behind her. Now, if she could only shake the nagging feeling that someone was watching her.

Common sense told her the creepy, goose bump–inciting feeling that she was being observed was totally unfounded, but that didn't make it any less real.

Determined to regain her former unflappable bravado, she gave herself a mental shake. There was absolutely no reason to be jumpy out here. She was hundreds of miles away from civilization, utterly alone in this remote stretch of wilderness. Her overactive imagination was simply playing tricks on her.

With her fears allayed by her inner voice of reason, she gave herself permission to get lost in the beauty surrounding her. Crouching behind a fallen log, she settled in to wait for a subject to feature in her next series of photos.

She didn't have to wait long. A loud *whoosh* broke the tranquil silence as a pileated woodpecker swooped in to land on a nearby fir tree. His massive black-and-white body was accented by a jaunty cap of red feathers, and his elongated beak and bright yellow eyes gave him a prehistoric appearance.

Focusing her camera on the big bird, she captured a flurry of images until the woodpecker halted his rhythmic drumming on the tree and abruptly took flight, the graceful flapping of his enormous wings propelling him deeper into the woods.

Catching sight of the reason for his hasty departure, an awestruck sigh escaped her lips. A handsome buck was emerging from the woods. Ears swiveling, the animal raised his head to sniff the air. His white tail flicked once, twice, before he gave in to temptation and began to feast on the tender blades of grass that had lured him from the depths of the forest.

Caught up in the magical moment, she framed the deer in her viewfinder and took the shot. Enchanted, she continued to click away. She didn't realize she'd lost track of time until the buck suddenly started, snapping to attention. Ears twitching, he looked straight at her and blew a warning through flared nostrils before bounding back into the woods from which he'd come.

Aware of the broody clouds that had gathered, warning of an approaching storm, and the lengthening shadows signaling dusk was settling in, Abbie decided it was time to head back to her cabin.

She'd stowed her gear in her backpack and was fastening it closed when a rustling in the nearby underbrush shattered the peaceful stillness enveloping her. Pausing midzip, her heart thumped against her ribs as she scanned her surroundings for the source of the disturbance.

Zeroing in on the cause of the commotion, she froze. She was being watched after all.

In a clearing just a few yards away, a bobcat's predatory gaze was fixed on her unwaveringly. The big cat challenging her to a stare down was easily forty pounds of finely honed muscle, armed with sharp claws and teeth. She'd be worried if she didn't know these wild cats weren't inclined to attack humans.

Despite the dwindling daylight and the ominous clouds marching darkly in her direction, excitement edged out her trepidation. There was no way she was leaving without photographing this glorious animal.

Retrieving her camera from her pack, she skillfully lined up the shot. Her delight at the unexpected up-close and personal photo opportunity morphed to stunned disbelief when she zoomed in on the majestic feline only to discover the bobcat wasn't the only subject filling her camera lens. The sharpened image highlighted something her naked eye hadn't seen—a quartet of shadowy figures, unmistakably human, silhouetted in the distance.

With an expert twist of a camera dial, she brought the blurry figures into focus. A jolt of recognition sent her pulse skittering in astonishment. One of the men bore an uncanny resemblance to New York business magnate Vince Romola. But what would the shady tycoon be doing out here in the middle of nowhere? Her eyes had to be playing tricks on her.

Hands trembling, she hurriedly adjusted the zoom. Her stomach lurched as the magnified image in her viewfinder sprang into sharp relief. Her eyes hadn't deceived her. It *was* Vince. The man who had destroyed her career.

When she'd worked as an investigative photojournalist, collecting a few enemies had been inevitable. The job wasn't exactly conducive to making friends and influencing people. Vince was the most dangerous of those adversaries. She'd been certain the son of a suspected mob boss was embroiled in the family business, and she'd set out to prove it.

After her editor had refused to let her pursue an exposé on Vince's misdeeds, citing insufficient proof, she'd decided to poke around on her own, hoping to find concrete evidence her boss wouldn't be able to ignore.

Her plan had backfired when Vince had caught on to her investigation. Though she hadn't gotten her hands on any substantial evidence to prove the unscrupulous entrepreneur was up to his neck in criminal activities, the severity of Vince's hair-trigger reaction when he'd discovered she'd been digging into his shady dealings had told her she'd gotten too close to the truth.

In setting out to strip away Vince Romola's cloak of false magnanimity and reveal the crimes he kept veiled behind his altruistic smokescreen, she'd poked the beast. Her David-vs.-Goliath scenario hadn't gone at all the way she'd planned. This Goliath had connections in places she'd never considered possible. She may have dealt a small blow against his corrupt empire, but he'd crushed her. He'd launched a completely unfounded smear attack against her, and he hadn't relented until he'd succeeded in torpedoing her career.

And then his twin brother, Vito Romola, had made a terrifying bid to end her life.

She had no idea what had brought Vince to this secluded stretch of wilderness. Whatever it was, it couldn't be good. The corrupt weasel didn't know the meaning of the word. He was the slickest of the slick, hiding his illegal dealings behind a veneer of polished professionalism in a well-practiced, upstanding-member-of-the-community act.

She was used to running toward trouble, not hiding from it, but she'd learned the hard way just how powerful Vince's network of influential associates was. And her brush with death at the hands of his twin had left her spirit crushed and altered her view of what mattered most in life.

If it hadn't been for the torturous ordeal Vito had put her through, she would have fought harder to prove his brother was chin-deep in dirty dealings. She had different priorities now, and none of them involved Vince Romola. Whatever illicit activity had landed him here, it was no longer her job to bring it to light. Vince had seen to that.

She'd never forget the vitriol in Vince's voice and the fury roiling in his eyes when he'd sought her out shortly after her release from the hospital to make sure she'd gotten the message that if she didn't stop digging around in his business, she would regret it.

Vince's unexpected appearance here, now, in the same stretch of Maine wilderness she'd taken refuge in, was disconcerting. Was it just a coincidence, or was he stalking her? The idea that it could be the latter made her blood run cold. She might not have been able to prove that he and his father were dirty, but she knew they were capable of anything—including murder.

If Vince *was* here looking for her, then he had a surprise coming. She wasn't going to tuck her tail between her legs and run. She wasn't going to let him chase her out of this wilderness haven. She wasn't going to let Vince's poisonous brand of evil threaten her first shot at normalcy since his serial-killer brother had tried to make her his next victim.

This stretch of wilderness was as widespread as it was secluded. She would simply avoid crossing paths with the criminal mastermind who'd invaded her sanctuary until he was done conducting whatever nefarious business had brought him here. Then, she would go back to trying to resurrect her life. She hadn't fully recovered from the injuries Vito had inflicted, and she needed this time here to heal both physically and emotionally. Spiritually, too. Her faith had taken a direct hit as a result of the incident that had almost ended her life.

She'd lost her way for a time after the attack, allowing all the *why me*s and *what-if*s to stand between her and her relationship with God. But she'd begun knitting that most precious of all relationships back together again. She was determined to claw her way out of the dismal abyss into which she'd plunged.

And she was working on letting go of the past.

Returning her focus to the bobcat, she snapped a series of photos until the big feline tired of his moment in the spotlight and turned and ambled away.

Satisfied with the pictures she'd shot, she slowly rose from her crouched position. Her leg muscles, still mending from the vicious knife wounds her abductor had inflicted, protested the action.

Pointing her camera toward the quartet in the distance, she checked to make sure her movements hadn't alerted Vince and his entourage to her presence. Though it felt like Vince was staring right through her, it was clear his attention was focused on a map spread out over the hood of a black Jeep that he and his companions were poring over.

As she watched, Vince moved to the back of the vehicle. He returned carrying an armful of rifles. Her heart slammed against her rib cage as he began distributing the weapons to his companions. It appeared he and his cohorts were about to embark on a hunting expedition. Her gut told her they weren't after any of the four-legged game that roamed these woods. She had a terrible feeling the quarry they were tracking was of the two-legged variety.

Her suspicions were confirmed when she saw Vince pull a photograph from his vest pocket. Focusing her camera lens on the image, she saw her own face staring back at her.

Her heart leaped to her throat as she fought hard to suppress the panic threatening to engulf her. She'd run from the fight, but now the fight had come to her. Her sanctuary was about to become a battlefield.

Ethan Knight loathed surprises. A phone call from his best friend and former coworker, Jaret Striker, would have been the exception to the rule had his buddy been reaching out merely to chat. Unfortunately, the New York Police Department detective's call wasn't a social one. It was a call to duty.

Listening intently as Jaret brought him up to speed on the threat that was about to come crashing down on the fortress of solitude he'd eked out here in the deep woods of Maine, Ethan fought to suppress his frustration and dismay. When he'd been a big-city detective, he'd spent his days and nights steeped in an ongoing battle against crime and corruption. He'd had his share of victories, but the defeats had far outweighed the wins. Every fresh loss had pierced him to his very soul. The weightiest of those losses was his inability to bring suspected mob boss Edgar Romola to justice, and his failure to stop Edgar's son Vito's reign of terror before the twisted serial killer claimed yet another victim in the same calculated, cold-blooded way he'd snuffed out his NYPD partner Gabriella Fernandez's life.

Desperate to break free from the riptide of senseless wrongdoings and exploitation before he drowned in a sea of disillusionment and cynicism, he'd turned in his detective's shield and headed for the Maine backcountry to carve out a new life for himself as a game warden. He'd found peace here in the seclusion of the wilderness. Now, his friend was asking him to dive back into the war he'd withdrawn from. A war against the very family that had torn his world apart, changing his life irrevocably.

Jaret's concerned voice cut into his ruminations. "Are you still there, pal?"

"Yeah. I'm here. I'm just trying to process everything. I'm finding your source's claim that the Romola family has chosen the northernmost wilderness of Maine as the next expansion spot for their drug business a little hard to swallow. Are you sure your informant has his facts straight?"

"His intel has always been ironclad. He swears the Romola family has boots on the ground in your neck of the woods. I believe him. He also maintains the Romolas have another reason for setting up shop there—he says they're out to eliminate a woman who's become a thorn in their side. Word is they plan to move quickly to execute the hit. We've got a ticking-time-bomb situation on our hands, and I need your help. We've already secured your lieutenant's approval. He says the decision to accept the mission is up to you, since you're due to start a week's vacation at the end of your shift today."

Ethan hesitated, torn. His indecision had nothing to do with his reluctance to postpone his vacation. The Spitting Image Slayer, the twisted malefactor who'd killed his NYPD partner, was the son of alleged crime boss Edgar Romola. That made this case far too personal for him. If he took it on, he'd be walking a fine line between justice and vengeance. He was afraid he'd land on the wrong side of that fight.

The knowledge that an innocent person was in jeopardy sliced through his gut like a knife. The thought of refusing his friend cut just as sharply. But there was no way he could get involved, no matter how badly he wanted to. He was passionate about following his call to protect and serve, but he was one failure away from never being able to claw his way back to being able to perform his job effectively. Another defeat would destroy him.

Ethan breathed a heavy sigh. "I'm sorry, Jaret, but I can't help. You, of all people, should know why I'm the wrong person for this fight."

Jaret's exasperated groan resounded in his ear. "When are you going to get it through that thick skull of yours that you're not responsible for what happened that night? You derailed a demented killer's rampage and you saved a life. I get that another life was lost. That's on Vito Romola, not on you."

Ethan's blue eyes shuttered as he winced at the unmerited praise. Prior to Vito Romola being exposed as the monster whose murderous rampage had spread fear throughout New York, the press had dubbed the serial killer the Spitting Image Slayer because of his twisted ritual of abducting a pair of women nearly identical in appearance, then forcing them to don matching dresses before murdering them and burying them in side-by-side graves.

After months of doggedly pursuing every lead only to have them dead-end, Ethan had finally gotten a tip that had led him to the killer. To his utter dismay, he hadn't arrived in time to prevent another tragedy.

Because of his failure, an innocent woman's life was lost, and another's was irrevocably altered when Vito carved the cross-hatching of knife cuts that was his calling card into her leg, leaving her scarred for life.

His botched attempt at serving and protecting had sliced ruts into his psyche as deep as the wounds the Slayer had inflicted on his victims. If those mental scars weren't enough of a reminder of his shortcomings, living with the knowledge that he'd failed to prevent the Spitting Image Slayer from being shot in cold blood while he was in his custody had been the death blow. That trifecta of failures haunted him to this day.

"I appreciate the vote of confidence, but the answer's still no," he maintained firmly.

The pause that followed was fraught with tension, as was Jaret's response. "There's something else you need to know. The Romola family's intended target is Abbie Renforth."

Ethan sucked in a stunned breath. The pulse in his jaw jumped, his blood heating in fury at the thought of anyone threatening the woman who was the only surviving victim of the Spitting Image Slayer's savage rampages.

The woman he'd saved, and whose quiet strength in the face of an unspeakable ordeal had left him with a deep respect for her strength and resilience.

He plowed a hand through his dark hair. "What do they want with Abbie? Vince Romola ended her career. His twin brother, Vito, almost ended her life. Haven't they put her through enough?"

"I don't get why they're targeting her, either. Retribution, maybe? Abbie's investigation into Vince's business dealings drew scrutiny the Romola family couldn't afford. Before Vince had her fired, her probings into his transactions dealt a crippling blow to one of the most lucrative branches of their business. What I do know for certain is that the hit to their bottom line got Edgar's attention, too, and now Vince and Edgar are out for blood. Abbie doesn't have a clue they've placed a target on her back. Someone has to warn her."

Ethan was silent for a long moment before replying. "There isn't anyone in your department who can get word to her?"

"We tried. She wasn't home when the detectives we sent to alert her about the threat arrived at her apartment. A neighbor told them Abbie is spending the summer in Maine, taking part in an artist-in-residence program. The woman had a cell phone number for Abbie, but the place she's staying at is so remote there's no cell reception. We're going to have to make contact in person. Normally we would send a helicopter, but there's a storm brewing and we can't risk putting a bird up. The nearest law enforcement officials are four hours away by ground. You're closer."

Pacing, Ethan rubbed the back of his neck. The Romolas were the embodiment of evil with a capital *E*. They had also proven to be untouchable. They'd perfected their upstanding-members-of-the-community act, but their altruistic deeds were only a cover for the myriad of illegal dealings upon which their unscrupulous empire was built.

Torn by indecision, Ethan hesitated. His past failures made him the last person on earth who should be racing to anyone's rescue, but if he refused to help, there could very well be devastating consequences. He was one hundred percent certain he wasn't the right person for this mission, yet how could he turn his back on an innocent young woman who'd already suffered the unthinkable?

Pressing his fingers into the muscles of his neck again, he heaved a sigh. "Text me with her location. I'll head there immediately."

Jaret's reply tumbled out in an outpouring of relief. "Thanks, pal. I appreciate it."

"You'd do the same for me. What's the plan once I locate her?"

"You'll need to find a safe place to lie low with her until the weather improves enough for us to take her to our safe house. The cabin she was provided by the artist-in-residence program is too easily discoverable. She can't stay there."

"The Warden Service has a chalet in the mountains that will work."

"Great. I'll text you with a link to our secure portal so you can send me the directions. I'll meet you there to take over her protection as soon as I can." Jaret paused a beat before continuing. "Just so you know, there's no one I'd rather have partnering with me on this assignment than you."

"I'll do my best to live up to your faith in me. I'll be in touch as soon as I locate her."

Hanging up the phone, Ethan sagged under the weight of the responsibility sitting heavily on his shoulders. Shaking off the overwhelming dread that Jaret's trust in him was misplaced, he said a prayer for Abbie's safety. He added a fervent request for the wisdom to deal with whatever circumstances he might face over the next few hours. He couldn't make even half a misstep on this mission. Abbie's life depended on it.

She thought he was a hero because he'd ended Vito Romola's reign of terror and saved her life, but he wasn't a hero. It was a wonder things hadn't ended far differently the night he'd rescued her.

To this day, he didn't have a clue who'd reached out to him with an anonymous tip informing him the Spitting Image Slayer was about to strike again. The caller had provided him with intimate details of the Slayer's plans, right down to the location of the forest outside the city where Vito had taken his latest pair of intended victims.

His decision to check out the tip on his own that night had been a purposeful one. The first time he'd gotten close to nabbing the Spitting Image Slayer, the killer had ambushed his partner, Gabriella, taking her hostage and using her as a human shield to avoid capture. Unable to get a clear shot at him, Ethan had watched in horror as the monster had fled with her. The Slayer had shoved Gabriella over an embankment into the Bronx River to her death as soon as he'd made it out of striking range. Her body had never been recovered.

Ethan had tracked his partner's killer relentlessly, but the Spitting Image Slayer had eluded capture. Months later, when he'd received an anonymous call tipping him off on the serial killer's whereabouts, he'd resolved to do everything in his power to ensure his second encounter with the felon ended differently. And it had.

He'd gotten the jump on the Slayer. The killer had meekly complied with his directive to toss down his knife and drop to the ground. Apprehending him had been easy. Too easy.

After cuffing his prisoner to a tree, Ethan had raced to the crudely dug, side-by-side graves where two women lay in blood-soaked dresses. They shared the same delicate facial features and wavy brunette hair and could easily have been mistaken for twins. Falling to his knees beside them, he'd desperately checked for signs of life only to find he'd arrived too late to save one of them.

He'd called for backup and an ambulance for the victim who was barely clinging to life. After doing his best to stabilize the survivor, he'd turned his attention back to the man in his custody. His rage had threatened to boil over, and it had taken every ounce of self-control he possessed not to stoop to the killer's level as he'd ripped off the man's mask. Astonishingly, he'd found himself eye to eye with Vito Romola, the son of suspected crime boss Edgar Romola.

Vito hadn't been the only menace lurking in the darkness, though. In his zeal to avenge Gabriella, Ethan had failed to clock the other threat until a gunshot ripped through the night. A single bullet from an unseen assailant's rifle had taken Vito out.

The blame for that lay squarely on him. And he had to live with the knowledge that he and Abbie were alive today not because of any heroic action on his part, but because, for whatever reason, the shooter had decided to spare them.

Shaking off the soul-lancing memories, he phoned his lieutenant to tell him he was delaying his vacation and accepting the assignment. He didn't want to tear the scab off Abbie's healing wound. He hated that he would have to break the news to her that the nightmare she was fighting her way back from had a sequel. But there was no other alternative.

Conscious of the urgent need to reach her before Romola and his men tracked her down, he grabbed his go bag and headed for the kennel to collect his partner, Zane. The K-9 greeted him with an exuberant woof, bounding up and down in an excited happy dance.

Grateful for the distraction, Ethan ruffled the German shepherd's thick coat affectionately. "Ready to go to work, buddy?"

Chuckling as the dog responded with a bark that confirmed he was not only ready but eager, Ethan opened the passenger-side door of his patrol truck and gave Zane the signal to jump into the vehicle.

His K-9 didn't need to be told twice. Road trips were at the top of the dog's list of favorite things to do, right up there with chasing squirrels and downing treats. He leaped into the passenger seat with a delighted doggie grin.

Focused on reaching Abbie as quickly as possible, Ethan hit the road. Pushing his speed past the prudent mark, he made the hour-and-a-half-long trip in just over an hour.

Following Jaret's directions, he reached the turnoff to the cabin where Abbie was staying and followed the side road to the house. His stomach nose-dived when he spotted the car registered to her parked in the driveway. The tires had been slashed.

His concern mounted when he saw the broken windowpane beside the front door. He'd been banking on reaching Abbie before the Romolas did. He feared they'd made it to her first.

Sensing his worry, Zane whined. Hastily exiting the truck, Ethan opened the door for his K-9 partner. Grabbing the dog's vest, he secured it around him.

Unholstering his Glock, he moved to the cabin entrance with the German shepherd at his side. Fractured shards of glass clung to the window the intruder had broken to gain access to the door lock.

Cautiously pushing the door open, Ethan whistled under his breath. The place had been violently ransacked. Quickly clearing each room, he found the cabin was empty. Holstering his weapon, he took stock of the damage.

The cabin's interior looked like it had been hit by a tornado. The sheer amount of destruction pointed to more than one person being involved in the break-in. Every nook and cranny of the space had been thoroughly rifled through.

Pots, pans, utensils and pantry items littered the kitchen floor. Books, swept off the floor-to-ceiling bookcases that once housed them, lay strewn across the living room's hardwood floor. In the primary bedroom, drawers were overturned and their contents left in disarray. The closet had been emptied, the clothes flung all across the room. Chunks of stuffing jutted from the slashed mattress.

The thoroughness with which the interior had been tossed told him the intruders had been looking for something. But what? They'd turned the place inside out searching for it, so it was likely Abbie hadn't been home when the break-in occurred. Either that or she'd fled when she saw them coming.

Spotting a silky sleep shirt draped over the bed, Ethan picked it up. A warm vanilla fragrance clung to the soft fabric. He offered the garment to Zane to sniff.

Among his many talents, the K-9 was an expert tracker, a skill that came in handy in the rugged terrain of the Maine woods, where hikers could easily veer off the marked trails and become lost. Satisfied the dog had Abbie's scent, Ethan brought him to the edge of the woods outside the cabin and took off his lead to give him the freedom to search the dense forest without constraint.

"Suke!" Ethan called out, giving his K-9 partner the command to track.

Muzzle to the air, Zane sniffed intently. His nose twitched as he caught Abbie's scent. Bounding ahead, he darted through the trees in pursuit of his quarry.

Running to keep pace with the dog, Ethan prayed they'd find Abbie before the men who'd ransacked her cabin did. At a divergence in the forest trail, Zane veered to the left and took off like a shot, disappearing around a bend. A moment later, his deep bark rang out.

Ethan's knees buckled in relief when he rounded the turn to see his dog sitting at Abbie's feet. His relief was replaced by horror when he spotted the glowing red dot hovering beside her, rapidly approaching her chest. Someone had her in their sights!

"Abbie!" he shouted.

His warning sounded at the exact moment the crack of a rifle shot reverberated through the air. Startled by his cry, Abbie took a step back. Her swift shift of position ensured the bullet missed its mark. Whizzing past her, it smacked into a nearby pine with a resounding crack.

Amid the barrage of wood splinters flying through the air, Ethan saw the laser dot homing in on Abbie again. Desperate to close the gap separating them, Ethan broke into a sprint. He had to reach her before the gunman lined up his next shot!

Abbie was only a few yards away, but the distance seemed like light-years. His stomach contorted when the boom of another rifle blast rang out. Jaw hardened in resolution, he launched himself toward her.

He'd failed her once. He couldn't fail her again.

TWO

No fear. Trapped in an unseen assailant's sights, the watch words that had once been Abbie's mantra of strength rang hollow. There'd been a time when she'd foolishly thought herself invulnerable, but she'd been fearless one time too many. She'd learned the hard way she wasn't unbreakable. First Vince Romola, and then his brother, Vito, had stripped her of her former bravado.

She'd come here to heal, and to reclaim her life. She'd never dreamed her newfound oasis of solitude would morph into a battlefield. Why was Vince Romola targeting her? And what was Ethan Knight doing here after he'd vanished from her life as unexpectedly as he'd entered it? How had he known she was in danger?

The questions ping-ponging through her brain were vaporized by the blast of another rifle shot. Returning fire, Ethan catapulted himself toward her and gently tumbled her to the ground, where a cushioning bed of pine needles broke her fall.

Acutely aware of the heavy press of her unexpected savior's muscular body wrapped around her like a shield, her panic subsided. Calmed by his solid warmth and the woodsy scent of his cologne, her breathing steadied. She wasn't alone in this fight any longer.

Beside them, a German shepherd crouched at the ready, hackles raised. Expecting to hear more gunshots at any moment, Abbie held her breath as her pulse thrummed in her ear like it was trying to break the sound barrier.

After what seemed like an eternity, the crunch of snapping twigs and the rustle of leaves crackling underfoot marked the shooter's hurried retreat.

No sooner had silence settled around them then the angry clouds chose that moment to burst open, sending raindrops pelting down on them. A flash of lightning streaked across the murky sky, highlighting Ethan's handsome face as he shifted off her.

"Are you okay?" he asked, his voice thick with concern.

She offered a tremulous smile. She'd heard that same worried tone lacing his deep voice when she'd regained consciousness in the hospital after the attack to find him keeping watch by her bedside. "Thanks to you, yes. It seems like saving my life is becoming a habit for you."

She'd never forgotten the compassion Ethan had shown her after he'd rescued her from the Spitting Image Slayer. He'd gone far above and beyond the call of duty. He'd ridden in the ambulance with her on the way to the hospital, murmuring words of reassurance. After learning she had no family, he'd stayed with her so she wouldn't wake up alone after the surgery that had repaired the multitude of knife slashes in her left leg.

He'd visited her often in the ensuing weeks of her recovery, carving out time in his busy schedule to cheer her on through the seemingly endless rounds of arduous physical therapy.

And then he'd disappeared from her life as quickly as he'd entered it.

"Don't thank me yet," he murmured wryly, drawing her from her thoughts. "I think the gunman fell back because one of my shots winged him. My guess is he isn't alone. If he does have accomplices, they'll have heard the exchange of gunfire. It won't be long before they show up. My truck is parked at your cabin. We need to get back there ASAP."

Offering her his hand, he helped her to her feet before introducing her to his K-9 partner. "This is Zane. I'm going to have him lead the way. He'll alert us if he senses anything off."

At the sound of his name, the big dog wagged his tail. Nodding his handsome head toward her, he woofed gently. For a moment, the interaction made her forget the direness of her situation before reality came stampeding back. "I'm glad you're both here, but I don't understand what's going on. Before someone took a shot at me just now, I saw Vince Romola in the woods with a group of armed men. I know he's behind this, but I don't understand why he's targeting me. I'm not an investigative reporter any longer. I'm not a threat to him."

Ethan raked a hand through his dark waves, his piercing blue eyes locking with hers. "I promise I'll explain everything as soon as we're on the road. Right now, the priority is getting you to safety. Your cabin isn't secure any longer—the men that are after you found it and ransacked it. The NYPD is sending a detective to escort you to one of their safe houses in New York."

"That doesn't explain how you're involved. From the uniform you're sporting, it seems you're a game warden now."

"Yes. But I've been called in to help the NYPD. Their safe house is a seven-hour drive away. Normally they would fly you there, but the current storm front has taken that option off the table. Since I'm the closest law enforcement officer to you, they asked me to find you and protect you until the weather improves enough for them to send a helicopter. We'll shelter at a chalet in the mountains that belongs to the Warden Service until they can get here."

Abbie fought back the tears threatening to flow. She was just beginning to piece the shattered remnants of her life back together. How could something like this be happening?

She'd come to Maine to lick her wounds and heal. She was making strides, but the few shards of memories she'd retained of the assault still had the power to leave her gutted every time they ran through her head. She wanted nothing more than to expunge the horrible recollection of the Slayer plunging his blade into her skin while she screamed in anguished terror. She wanted to cling to the peace she'd found in this remote wilderness refuge. She didn't want to leave. But Ethan was right. She wasn't safe here any longer.

The trek back to the cabin in the pouring rain was miserable. Her injured leg was still healing, so the stiffness in her muscles made keeping up with Zane's swift pace challenging. Soon, her steps began to flag.

"We're almost there," Ethan encouraged her. "Stick close to me."

The rain fell harder, pouring down on them in unrelenting torrents. The cold, wind-driven drops pelted her skin and obscured her vision. Conscious of the need to get to shelter sooner rather than later, she forced herself to press forward, concentrating on putting one foot in front of the other.

"What happens next?" she asked, needing to focus on something other than her screaming muscles and her chilled and soggy state.

"When we reach the cabin, I want you to wait in my truck with Zane while I go in and make sure the place is secure. Once I'm sure the intruders haven't circled back, you can pack a bag. I'm afraid you may have to dig around a bit to find what you need. The men who broke into your place combed through your belongings pretty thoroughly."

Grateful for Ethan's presence, a familiar face during this storm, but rattled by the surreal turn of events all the same, Abbie shivered involuntarily. "Why would they do that?"

"I don't know, but I promise you I'm going to get to the bottom of this."

Abbie's eyes burned with intent as her gaze collided with Ethan's. If Ethan thought she was going to stand by and do nothing while he risked his life for her again, he was mistaken. "*We'll* get to the bottom of this. There's no way I'm going to let Vince ruin my life again—or worse. If you're going after him, I'm going with you."

Ethan had spent a great deal of time considering how best to break the news to Abbie about the situation she was facing. How did he tell her the man who'd robbed her of the career she'd poured her heart and soul into now wanted to take even more from her, and that Vince's father shared his goal to destroy her life?

Abbie had solved that problem for him with her assertion that Vince was involved. "You're right about Vince," he confirmed, compassion thickening his voice.

Her green eyes sparked with indignation. "When I first saw him, I thought he might be chasing down some drug dealer who had crossed him. I can't believe he's after *me*. He's already destroyed my career. What more could he possibly want?"

"I'm afraid I don't know. Whatever it is that he's after, I guarantee you I'm not going to let him get it."

Ethan paused, considering what to say next. His heart ached for what she was being forced to face. Figuring out how to soften the blow when he told her the Romola family wanted her dead wasn't the only thing that had been weighing heavily on his mind. He'd spent a great deal of time pondering the apology he owed her for abruptly dropping out of her life after she was released from the hospital.

He regretted not responding to her calls and text messages after he'd left New York, but he'd done it for her own good. He'd made the mistake of letting the lines between professional and personal blur and had begun to think of her as a friend—something that was positively off-limits in his book. Afraid she'd begun to see him in that same light, too, he'd had no choice but to reestablish the boundaries between them. He wasn't friend material. Anyone he let close always wound up getting hurt.

Zane was approaching the trailhead that opened out to the cabin, now, so his apology was going to have to wait. Quietly commanding the dog to halt, he grabbed a pair of mini binoculars from his belt and scanned the surroundings for any signs the intruders had returned.

Turning to Abbie, he shot her a reassuring smile. "Everything looks secure. I don't think anyone has been back, but I'm going to sweep the interior before you go inside just to play it safe."

Reaching his truck, Ethan opened the passenger-side door and ushered Abbie and Zane into the vehicle. After locking it, he rounded the hood and drew his gun before heading to the cabin.

After checking all the rooms and finding the place empty, he returned to the truck and opened the door for her. "It's all clear. You can get your things now."

While he guarded the cabin, Abbie swiftly gathered her belongings with Zane as her shadow. Though Ethan's attention was zeroed in on the entry points, monitoring for any sign of trouble, the occasional glimpse he caught of her as she packed expediently and efficiently had him admiring her composure.

When she'd gotten her first glimpse of the disaster the intruders had left in their wake, the color had drained from her face. She'd recovered quickly, showing the same remarkable strength in the face of adversity as she had the night he'd rescued her.

Now, as she returned from the bedroom with her purse slung over her shoulder and carrying a travel bag, her lips curved in a tremulous smile. "Okay. I'm ready. I wish I could clean up and change into some dry clothes before we go, but I know that's not an option."

"I wish it was, but the clock is ticking. It's only a matter of time before Vince and his men regroup. This will be one of the first places they come looking for you. There's no time to clean up, but we can spare a few minutes for you to change."

She flashed another smile, this one markedly brighter. "I was hoping you'd say that. I'll be right back."

He sent Zane with her again while he continued to stand guard. She returned a few minutes later, having swapped her soaked garments for jeans and a long-sleeved violet T-shirt.

"This is so much better." Pausing, she gestured at his sodden uniform. "What about you? Do you have anything with you that you can change into?"

"I keep a spare shirt in my vehicle, but I'm fine. Getting drenched goes along with the territory in this job. Are you ready to brave the storm and make a run for the truck?"

"My leg has reached its limits, so it will be more like a fast walk for me at this point, but let's do it," she affirmed with a determined nod.

After conducting another visual sweep of the perimeter, Ethan led the way to his truck. Opening the door for Abbie, he saw her safely seated before letting Zane in the back.

Taking his place behind the wheel, he started the engine. As he drove down the secluded camp road, he remained on the lookout for any suspicious activity. Nothing set off his internal alarm bells, much to his relief.

Soon, they reached the intersection where the camp road met the main drive. Shiny from the heavily falling rain, the paved surface stretched ahead of them like a glossy black ribbon. He turned onto the route, heading north toward the mountains and the Warden Service's chalet. Abbie would be safe there.

"Harmony Cove is only about an hour away. We can stop and get a bite to eat and rest," he relayed. Scanning the road ahead, he was relieved to see it was free of traffic. His eyes flicked to the rearview mirror and met the reassuring sight of nothing behind them but blue-black darkness, pierced by the occasional lightning bolt that highlighted the driving rain.

Confident they weren't being followed, he let himself relax a bit. His stress returned tenfold when he contemplated the conversation he needed to have with Abbie. The apology she was due remained lodged in his throat, and that wasn't fair to her. She deserved an explanation for why he'd ghosted her after her release from the hospital. He wasn't proud of how he'd left things between them, but he'd walked away because it was best for her in the long run. He really needed her to understand that.

"I owe you an apology," he began, hesitating as he considered what to say next. "I'm sorry for ignoring your calls and texts. It was wrong of me to drop out of your life like I did."

Her eyes snapped to his, surprise welling in their emerald green depths. "You have nothing to apologize for. Was I disappointed when you didn't return my calls and texts? Truthfully, yes. I thought we could be friends. Hoping we could be, actually. After a few weeks went by, I finally realized I'd read too much into the time you'd spent with me. You weren't looking to expand your social circle. You were just doing your job. I only wish you would have told me you were leaving before you disappeared from my life without a backward glance. Ghosting me the way you did hurt me more than if you'd told me the truth."

Ethan cringed. "It was an insensitive thing to do, and I'm truly sorry."

Abbie shrugged off his apology. "Don't worry about it. It's all water under the bridge, at any rate. Besides, it wasn't like I had anything to bring to a friendship. I was so wrapped up in trying to rebuild my life I didn't have anything to offer."

Ethan's eyebrows snapped together. Was that what she thought? That she had nothing to offer him? She had everything to offer. That was the problem. He didn't have anything to offer her in return.

Before he had a chance to utter a single word in response, he caught the glow of headlights out of the corner of his eye. His gaze snapped to the rearview mirror. Spotting a vehicle gaining on them rapidly, his mouth went dry. "I think we're being followed. It may be nothing, but I need to make sure. I'm going to speed up to see how they respond."

She nodded, turning to get a look at the vehicle trailing them. "It's a black Jeep like the one Vince and his men were standing by when I saw them earlier," she breathed. "There's only one guy in this vehicle, though. It could just be a coincidence."

"Hang on. We're about to find out." Pressing down on the accelerator, he sent his truck surging forward. The driver tailing them immediately matched the faster pace. Ethan's jaw tightened as the validity of the threat was confirmed. Trouble. There was going to be trouble.

Ethan hoped the look he shot Abbie communicated confidence rather than betraying the uncertainty he was feeling. They were in a tough spot. "I'm afraid he's definitely tailing us. If he makes a move, I won't be able to outrun him. This road is too narrow and winding to allow for any evasive driving maneuvers. With the embankment on your side and the cliff on mine, we're penned in." His eyes flicked to hers. "Have you ever fired a gun before?"

Abbie nodded. "I got a firearm and my concealed carry permit after I was attacked."

"Do you have your gun with you?"

"Yes. It's in my purse."

"Good. If things get sticky, I may need you to try and take out one of his tires. Are you comfortable with that?"

No sooner than he'd voiced the question, the Jeep gained momentum and drew up behind them. Stomping on the gas pedal again, Ethan sent his truck racing forward. The Jeep driver copied the maneuver. It was only a matter of time before the man pursuing them made his move.

Ethan's brow furrowed. "Roll your window down and have your gun ready in case things go south," he instructed Abbie.

Seeing the driver lining up to strike, Ethan swung the wheel sharply. Swerving back and forth as far as the narrow road would allow, he heard the whine of the Jeep's engine. The vehicle was close. Too close.

Ethan's hands contracted on the wheel. "Brace yourself," he warned Abbie.

The jolt came hard and fast, accompanied by the screeching crunch of metal abrading metal. It took every ounce of driving skill he possessed to prevent the truck from veering into the cliffside. Accelerating again, he managed to put space between them and the Jeep. His heart hammered in his chest as he realized it wasn't going to be enough.

He had two options, neither of them good. He could have Abbie try and take out one of the Jeep's tires, but between the speed they were traveling and the reduced visibility, that was a long shot at best. The only other play was to try and catch the driver off guard with a maneuver he wouldn't be expecting.

He had to make a decision pronto. The driver was speeding up to make another run at them. They were approaching a sharp curve ahead. He would only have one shot at the Hail Mary pass he was contemplating.

Sheets of rain lashed the windshield, obscuring his view of the road. Saying a prayer for their safety, he opted to attempt the risky maneuver he felt certain was their best hope for survival.

Racing toward the curve, Ethan jammed on the brakes the moment he reached the hairpin turn. Water from the deep puddles that had pooled on the road sprayed from his tires as he spun his truck around to face the Jeep. They were close enough to the vehicle now that they could see the driver's face. The man's features contorted with shock as he was forced to slam on his brakes.

Momentum was not the speeding Jeep driver's friend. In a squeal of sliding tires, the vehicle spun out of control on the rain-slick pavement. Ethan had hoped to halt the driver's progress, and he had. But rather than steer into the skid, the man failed to regain command of the vehicle.

The Jeep careened toward the guardrail, striking it at full speed. Catapulting over the steel barrier, the vehicle plummeted down the embankment in a series of horrendous airborne twists and turns before it crashed into the boulders at the bottom of the ravine with a sickening crunch of crumpling metal.

After making sure Abbie and Zane were okay, Ethan scrambled from his truck and raced to the driver's aid. He was halfway down the steep ravine when the flames licking at the wreckage ignited in a fiery explosion, the blast setting shock waves pulsating under his feet.

He wasn't aware Abbie had followed him until he heard her horrified gasp behind him. Turning, he saw her standing frozen in shock, her eyes wide with disbelief and her beautiful face devoid of color. "It's too late to save him, isn't it?" she murmured.

There was no way to soften the blow. Heart heavy with regret, he nodded solemnly. "I'm afraid so. Can you tell—was he one of the men you saw in the woods with Vince?"

Swallowing hard, she bobbed her head in confirmation as together they watched the one chance they might have had to glean answers from the driver go up in flames. Ethan was certain the blinding conflagration and the thick black smoke rising from the wreckage would be a beacon to Vince and his remaining associates. The men were undoubtedly still out there somewhere, planning their next attack.

He feared this battle had only begun.

THREE

Trembling in the aftermath of the terrifying chase and subsequent crash, Abbie gaped at the Jeep's burning remains. "I know that man intended to kill us, but his death is such a senseless loss. Things didn't have to end this way. I don't understand any of this. Why does Vince want to get at me so badly that he's willing to go to these extremes? Wasn't annihilating my career punishment enough? And what his brother did..." She trailed off, her voice catching on a sob.

Ethan shook his head, sadness sweeping across his face. "I wish I had the answers. Criminals aren't known for thinking rationally, I'm afraid."

"This is all so surreal. I dropped my investigation into Vince's illegal dealings months ago. There's no reason for him to come after me again. I never should have poked him in the first place by showing my hand before I had enough evidence to prove he was a key player in the Northeast drug trade. But the facts my source shared with me added up, and I was certain my editor would agree to let me chase down the story. Instead, he nixed it. I would have proceeded more cautiously if I'd known the Romola family had the newspapers in their pockets."

"The Romola family's influence has a wider reach than the media. Part of the reason they're so adept at circumventing the law is that they have a network of powerful people under their thumb in key places, including the NYPD. Their justice-evasion streak is about to end, though."

Drawing her to his side, Ethan guided her away from the ghastly scene. "We should get back on the road. The sooner we reach Harmony Cove, the sooner you'll be safe."

As if to reinforce his statement, a lightning bolt zigzagged across the cloud-burdened sky, followed by a jarring boom of thunder.

Together, they scrambled up the mud-slick incline. They'd almost reached the top when Abbie's foot slid, sending her skidding backward. Ethan hastily reached out to steady her, stopping her from tumbling down the hill. She flashed him a grateful smile.

Back on level ground, they made their way back to the truck. Ethan saw her seated in the vehicle, then checked on Zane before joining her.

"We're about an hour and a half away from my friend's place and the best barbecue you've ever tasted. My buddy Caleb moved to Maine after he retired from the NYPD. He and his wife, Sarah, settled in Harmony Cove and opened a restaurant and inn. Caleb is a pitmaster extraordinaire, and he grills all the meat and seafood dishes on the menu."

Abbie's stomach growled in anticipation of the yummy feast. "Sounds delicious!"

"As soon as we arrive at the inn, I'll book a couple of rooms so we can clean up and change into some dry clothes. I'll call in an anonymous tip on the accident to keep us out of the spotlight."

"I'm so glad you showed up when you did. The world needs more heroes like you."

"I'm not a hero, Abbie," he quickly countered, a flush of embarrassment creeping up his neck.

The vehement conviction, laced with sadness, in his tone took Abbie aback. Why was he so determined not to take credit for all the good he'd done? "You're wrong, you know. You are the very definition of a hero."

"If I'd actually made a difference when I worked for the NYPD, that might be true. But I didn't."

"I'm living proof you made a difference. I'm alive because of your heroism," she refuted softly.

"You give me more credit than I deserve. Truthfully, I messed up the night I rescued you. I made a mistake that could very well have cost you your life had things gone down differently."

Abbie frowned in confusion. "What do you mean?"

"My partner at the NYPD, Gabriella, died at Vito's hands. I was so intent on getting justice for her, I didn't realize Vito wasn't the only killer out there that night. The person who shot the Spitting Image Slayer could easily have taken you and me out, too. Your being alive today has nothing to do with any act of heroism on my part and everything to do with God's grace."

"The way I see it, God sent you. You'll always be a hero to me."

"That's praise I'm not worthy of. I didn't arrive in time to stop Vito from hurting you. I didn't prevent him from killing the other woman he abducted along with you, or the dozens of other victims he murdered before that night—including my own partner." Pausing, he sighed heavily before continuing. "I'm sure there are other victims who haven't been discovered yet. The families of those missing women will never have closure because someone took it upon themselves to silence Vito before he could be prosecuted. If I'd kept him safe, he would have stood trial. Justice would have been served, and those emotionally wounded families might have gotten answers."

"It's not your fault someone shot him. On the topic of answers, though, how did you find out the Romolas were after me? How did you know where to find me? You said you'd explain what was going on once we were on the road."

Ethan rubbed the back of his neck and sighed. "I'm still good friends with an NYPD detective, Jaret Striker. He's part of a special task force working to build a case against the Romola family, and they've been working diligently to build a case against Vince Romola. One of Jaret's informants contacted him with a tip that the Romola family was expanding their drug trade and that they'd chosen the northernmost wilderness of Maine to grow the business. The informant also told Jaret that Vince and Edgar see you as a threat—a threat they plan to mitigate."

"And by *mitigate* he means eliminate."

"Yeah, the Romolas want you out of the way permanently. They want to ensure you don't stir up trouble for them."

"But I can't. I honestly don't have any evidence proving they're a crime family. Vince had me ousted from my job before I could substantiate my source's allegations against him. I'm not a threat to him or his father."

* * *

Ethan's jaw tightened. The Romolas didn't see it that way. They were gunning for her. Taking one hand off the steering wheel, he laid it gently on Abbie's shoulder. "I'm not sure why you have them so rattled, but after what went down today, it's obvious they see you as a problem they need to deal with. Don't worry. I'm going to figure this out."

"*We'll* figure it out," she countered insistently, fixing him with a determined look.

He heaved a sigh. He wasn't about to let her leap into the fray with the stakes as high as they were. Removing his hand from her shoulder, he quickly changed the subject. He didn't want to engage in a verbal fencing match. "We're about an hour away from Harmony Cove. Why don't you see if you can get some rest?"

Abbie raised an eyebrow, her expression plainly conveying she knew he was deflecting to avoid the conversation. She didn't argue, though, and when he glanced in her direction a few minutes later, he saw her eyelids had drifted shut.

Her trust in him was humbling. He would die before he'd let any harm come to her, but that didn't make him the hero she claimed he was. A hero wouldn't have allowed his partner to be ambushed and murdered right in front of his eyes. A hero would have tracked down Vito Romola before he could kill again. A hero would have ensured the man was locked up for life for his crimes, not shot in cold blood on his watch.

He'd only driven a few miles when a deafening roar drowned out the booming thunder and rattled the ground beneath them. The cacophony intensified when a section of the cliff bordering the roadway came tumbling down, barricading the route they'd just traveled.

Startled awake, Abbie grabbed his arm reflexively. "Was that an earthquake?"

"No. That was an explosion. I saw a flash of light at the top of the hill as we passed it right before the blast. Vince and his crew must have expected us to take this route, but they're on the highway that runs above us. There's no access to this road from there for miles. They must have triggered the blast to stall us when they realized they couldn't reach us in time."

No sooner than he'd voiced the explanation, a second, much closer burst of light cut through the darkness. With an earsplitting roar, another explosion ripped through the cliff, shattering a huge chunk of the rock face directly ahead of them.

Ethan stamped down on the accelerator, urging his truck forward. Zigzagging back and forth, he navigated the tidal wave of rocks and boulders surging toward them.

"Look out!" Abbie warned, pointing to a huge slab of stone headed directly for the hood of the truck.

With a swift yank on the steering wheel, Ethan veered out of the boulder's path in the nick of time.

"That was close," Abbie breathed as they sped away from the remnants of the rockslide.

"Yeah. If they'd had another minute to set the charges, we would have been trapped." Pausing, he took his eyes off the road for a second to glance behind him. Zane sat calmly in his reinforced K-9 compartment, sporting a tongue-lolling grin that showcased his sharp white teeth. "Looks like Zane isn't fazed by our close call. Nothing shakes him. He's an awesome partner."

"I can tell that under that tough exterior he's just a big marshmallow. For what it's worth, I'm sorry you both got dragged into this mess."

Ethan's expression morphed to one of steely resolve. He would do whatever it took to keep Abbie safe. "It's my job. Zane's job, too."

"Speaking of jobs, I was surprised to see you traded in your detective's plain clothes for a game warden uniform. I thought you loved your career. Why did you decide to leave the NYPD?"

For a moment, Ethan was tempted to ignore the question. But he knew her well enough to realize that, like Zane latching on to his favorite chew toy, she wouldn't let go easily, so he offered up a succinct explanation. "I needed a change of pace."

To his relief, she didn't press. She dropped the subject in favor of circling back to the conversation he'd sidelined earlier.

"I'm not going to run from the Romola family," she reaffirmed. "There's absolutely no way I'm going to stand by twiddling my thumbs while you risk your life for me. I'll go with you to the safe house until we can regroup and forge a plan, but I'm not going to hide. I want to be a part of this. I want to help you prove the Romolas are up to their ears in illegal dealings."

Seeing the inferno of determination blazing in her beautiful green eyes, Ethan bit back the refusal that was on the tip of his tongue. Vince Romola had destroyed the career she'd poured her heart and soul into. His twin brother had put her through the unthinkable.

Abbie was tough. He had no doubt she'd heal from the physical and emotional wounds Vito had inflicted.

Still, her leg was marked by scars she'd carry with her forever—an ever-present reminder of the brutality she'd faced at the hands of the Spitting Image Slayer. He understood her need to take a stand.

Seeing that he was weighing his answer, Abbie doubled down on her argument. "I want to be part of this fight, Ethan. I realize I'm not a trained law enforcement officer, but I'm a skilled investigator. Let me help you put the Romolas behind bars where they belong."

Ethan scrubbed a hand across his face. He was undoubtedly making a colossal mistake by agreeing, but there was no way he could refuse her passionate entreaty. She needed to be a part of this, and he couldn't deny her that. "Okay. You can help. But when I say 'help,' that doesn't entail you rushing in at the front line where you'll be in danger. It means you can lend a hand chasing down the paper trail that will build a solid case against the Romolas. That's it."

Before she could get a word in edgewise, a jagged streak of lightning rent the clouds. With an earsplitting crack, the lightning bolt struck a massive pine. Dissected at its base, the towering evergreen began to fall. It was headed directly for them.

His stomach contorting, Ethan slammed on the brakes. Fighting to keep the truck from sliding out on the rain-drenched tarmac, he prayed he could bring the vehicle to a halt before the monstrous tree crushed them.

FOUR

Abbie recoiled in her seat, her breath seizing in her lungs as the massive pine tree bore down on them. The frantic tattooing of her zooming pulse in her ears drowned out the rasp of the pine's massive limbs as they scraped past the truck.

Crashing to the pavement in front of them with only inches to spare, the tree smacked the road with a quaking thud that sent shock waves reverberating through the vehicle.

If not for Ethan's quick reflexes, the tree would have pulverized them. Hearing him murmur a prayer of gratitude for their safety, Abbie added one of her own.

Uttering a heartfelt *amen*, Ethan turned to her, his brilliant blue eyes brimming with concern. "Are you okay?"

"I'm fine," she assured him. "Are you?"

He nodded, then turned to check on his K-9 partner. "You all right back there, Zane?"

The German shepherd woofed a reply that sounded a lot like "yup," making them both chuckle despite the gravity of their situation.

With the safety of his passengers confirmed, Ethan rolled down his window amid a shower of soggy evergreen needles to assess the state of the road ahead. The smell of charred wood drifted into the truck.

Afforded her first unobstructed view of the damage, Abbie sucked in a shocked breath. The section of the gigantic pine that had been bisected by the lightning bolt was in flames, and the tree couldn't have toppled at a worse angle. Its length and massive girth completely blocked the road.

"There's no way we can drive around it," she breathed in dismay.

"I'm going to make a way," Ethan assured her. "Stay here with Zane. I keep a fire extinguisher and a chain saw in the storage box in the truck bed. I'll have the road passable again in no time."

"Let me help. I can move the sections of tree you cut off the road."

Mouth set in a determined line, he shook his head. "Absolutely not. We have no idea where Vince and his associates are right now. This stretch of road is heavily wooded, with too many places for a shooter to hide. I need you to stay in the truck."

She didn't have a chance to argue the point. Stepping out into the gale, he grabbed the extinguisher and snuffed out the flames. Retrieving his chain saw, he brought the tool to life with a yank of the pull cord and set to work cutting up the fallen tree.

After quickly sawing the downed evergreen into logs and lugging them off the roadway, Ethan stowed his tools back in the storage compartment of the truck and rejoined her. Putting the truck in gear, he pointed it toward their destination. "Our next stop is Caleb and Sarah's, barring any more surprises," he announced with a wry grin.

"I think we've had enough of those for one day," Abbie chuckled.

His mouth curved in another smile, bringing his dimples springing into action. "Agreed."

The rain fell in torrents, all but obscuring the road. With the truck's headlights struggling to pierce the double-jeopardy combo of pitch-black darkness and blinding sheets of precipitation, it was no surprise they nearly missed their turnoff.

A bright flash of lightning illuminated the sign for the Sand Dune Inn and Smokehouse Restaurant just in time for Ethan to turn onto the driveway leading to the sprawling, saltbox-style farmhouse that housed his friends' business. Despite the horrific weather—or perhaps because of it—every spot in the large parking area was filled.

"Popular place," Abbie noted as Ethan drove through the packed lot.

"They've only been open for six months, but they've already earned a five-star rating. I can't wait for you to meet Caleb and Sarah. I know you're going to love them."

"Are you sure our stopping here is wise? With the Romolas determined to find me, maybe this isn't such a great idea. I don't want to drag anyone else into this mess, and there are a lot of guests here."

"I appreciate your concern, but it's okay. I texted Caleb earlier and brought him up to speed on the situation. He agrees our taking a time-out here is a smart move. Vince and his associates will have to cover a lot of miles to catch up with us. Even if they could make up the distance, there are dozens of exits along the way. They have no way of knowing whether we took one of them. If they try and locate us, they'll be facing a needle-in-a-haystack challenge."

Bypassing the general parking area, Ethan drove around to the back of the building and pulled into an open bay in a four-car garage attached to a smaller version of the charming farmhouse that housed the inn and restaurant. "Caleb suggested I park here so my truck won't be in plain sight if anyone should come poking around. It's unmarked, but the men who saw it will still easily recognize it."

Grabbing Zane's travel bed, collapsible bowls, kibble, and water, he created a cozy spot for the dog to wait while he and Abbie checked in with his friends. Satisfied Zane was comfortably settled, Ethan closed the garage door before he and Abbie hurried to the restaurant to get out of the rain. The moment they entered the inviting lobby, a handsome older man with salt-and-pepper hair greeted them.

"Ethan! It's great to see you!" the man enthused. "I was beginning to worry about you two."

"We were beginning to worry, too," Ethan replied with a wry grin. "We would have been here earlier, but we ran into a bit of trouble. Caleb, I'd like you to meet Abbie Renforth."

Abbie extended her hand. "It's a pleasure to meet you."

Ignoring her outstretched hand, Caleb drew her in for a hug. "Likewise," he told her with a warm smile. Releasing her, he turned his attention to Ethan, clasping his shoulder fondly. "This trouble you encountered on the way here, was it in the form of the Romolas or the storm?"

Ethan winced. "Both."

Caleb nodded sympathetically. "Then I'm sure you and

Abbie would appreciate a chance to clean up." Pulling a key from his pocket, he handed it to Ethan. "This is for the main house. Sarah and I insist you stay with us tonight."

Ethan's forehead furrowed. "We couldn't put you out like that," he replied, his gratitude for the offer reflected in his eyes. "We'll just book a couple of rooms."

"Nonsense," Caleb refuted firmly. "You're part of the family, and family stays with us. We have plenty of space."

Abbie didn't share Ethan's conviction that by staying here they weren't bringing trouble to Caleb and Sarah's door. She didn't try to mask her concern. "I don't want to lead the men that are after me to your door."

"Let Ethan and me worry about that," Caleb insisted gently. "If anyone comes looking for you here, they'll have to go through us to get to you. And Lucas."

"Lucas is Caleb and Sarah's German shepherd," Ethan explained. "He and Zane are best buddies."

"Go on up to our place and make yourselves comfortable," their host insisted. "Lucas stays in the sunroom while Sarah and I are working. Zane can join him there. When you and Abbie are ready for dinner, come back to the restaurant. I've saved our best table for you."

Abbie watched as Ethan patted their host's shoulder in gratitude for his hospitality. It was easy to see the bond the men shared ran deep.

"Thank you, Caleb. We appreciate it," Ethan responded warmly.

"No need to thank me. It's nothing compared to the debt I owe you," Caleb replied, wrapping an arm around Ethan's broad shoulders and turning to face her. "This guy saved my Sarah from a stalker. His quick action is the reason she's alive today. She's busy with the dinner crowd at the moment, but she's looking forward to meeting you, Abbie. As soon as the dinner rush is over, we'll join you and Ethan for dessert."

Stepping back out into the gale, they hurried to Caleb and Sarah's home. Ethan unlocked the door and ushered her inside before returning to the garage to collect Zane and their gear.

A few minutes later, he rejoined her in the cozy entryway and set their bags down. "I'll be right back. I'll just get Zane settled in with Lucas."

By the time she'd unlaced her hiking boots and toed out of them, Ethan had returned. "Is it okay if I go and clean up?" she asked.

"Of course. The guest rooms are upstairs. I'll stay down here and keep an eye on things. I'm not expecting any trouble, but there's no harm in being cautious."

The bedrooms on the second level were all equally inviting, featuring canopy beds made up with luxurious linens. She chose the room at the end of the hall, drawn to its lavender–and–forest green color scheme.

Closing the door, she slumped against it, taking a moment to just breathe. As the reality of not one but two close calls began to sink in, and the adrenaline that had carried her through dissipated, she felt the false bravado she'd been clinging to since everything had gone awry dropping away like peony blossoms in a deluge.

Determined not to give in to the urge to have a meltdown, she brushed away the tears that mingled with the water droplets dripping from her drenched hair. She'd endured far worse than what had transpired today. So why did she feel so off-balance and vulnerable?

Ethan was why.

Seeing him again so unexpectedly had come as a shock. She was grateful he'd found her in time to help her evade the Romolas' clutches, but if he thought she was going to go along meekly with his plan to tuck her away in a safe house while he and his law enforcement colleagues put their lives at risk, he was seriously mistaken. She was done running from the Romola family. She wasn't going to let them take more from her than they already had. She fully intended to play a role in ending their reign of terror—whether Ethan wanted her to be a part of this mission or not.

Sitting across the table from Abbie in his friends' cozy restaurant, Ethan allowed himself to let his guard down a bit for the first time since Jaret had contacted him. The fire crackling in the stone hearth and the candlelight flickering from candelabras in the center of the tables that were artfully arranged in the dining room to afford the best vantage to soak in the scenery invited relaxation. The nighttime view of the storm-riled ocean from the windows spanning the room was breathtaking.

What had begun this morning as a relatively benign assignment to locate Abbie and keep her out of harm's way until Jaret arrived to take over had unexpectedly escalated into a full-blown protection mission. There wasn't a doubt in Ethan's mind that, had he not happened on the scene when he had, Vince Romola and his men would have taken her out.

His orders only extended to finding Abbie and keeping her safe until Jaret could reach them, but he was going to ask to stay on as a member of the task force working to bring down the Romola family. If his request was denied, he would use the many weeks of vacation time he'd accumulated to assist with the mission.

He hadn't told Abbie about his plan to stay on yet. He wasn't sure how she'd take the news. He didn't want to mention it over dinner and ruin her enjoyment of the amazing pulled pork, slow-smoked ribs, black beans, rice and corn bread Caleb had prepared, or put a damper on their conversation. He was enjoying reconnecting with her.

When he'd dropped out of Abbie's life after she'd been released from the hospital, he'd convinced himself he was doing it for her own good. In his line of work, friendships were a liability. He didn't want to let anyone close only to see them get caught in the crossfire of hazards that went along with his profession.

He was used to shrugging off danger. Risk-taking, albeit the carefully calculated variety, was something he did without hesitation. But he was one hundred percent certain bringing Abbie into the equation would be a mistake. He couldn't chance a repeat of what had happened with Sondra.

He and Sondra had started out as friends, but that friendship had soon deepened to love. At least he'd thought it had.

Unable to come to terms with the stark realities of his chosen career, Sondra had checked out of their relationship—only she hadn't bothered to tell him how she really felt. She'd professed to love him, but she'd loved someone else more. He'd only discovered the truth after she'd left him standing at the altar.

After her rejection, he'd floundered in a morass of bitterness and anger. Eventually, he'd come to realize the dissolution of their relationship was for the best. If they had married, Sondra would have inevitably pressed him to choose between her and the work that was as important to him as the very air he breathed. She'd gone on to wed the man who had stolen her heart, and he'd remained in the career he loved. The breakup had ultimately brought him and Sondra more happiness than they ever could have had if they'd entered into a union that would have been built on unstable ground from the very start.

"This is so delicious," Abbie enthused. "Thanks for arranging this. And thank you for showing up when you did today."

Drawn from his reflections, Ethan glanced up at her. His breath caught in his throat as his gaze tangled with hers. The sunshine in her eyes overshadowed the darkness of the storm like a lighthouse beacon.

Giving himself a mental shake, he hastily deflected her gratitude. He'd done nothing to deserve it. "The credit for that goes to the NYPD. One of their confidential informants alerted them to the Romola family's plan to go after you. They reached out to me for help because I happened to be closest to your location."

"I'm still trying to wrap my mind around your career change. It was so apparent that the NYPD was in your blood."

"I loved working as a detective, but going up against men like Vito Romola extracts a price. The job was beginning to color the way I looked at humanity. When I realized I was starting to lose faith in my ability to make a difference, I decided it was time I chose a different path before I lost my passion for protecting and serving. I've always loved the outdoors, and the chance to work with a K-9 appealed to me. Becoming a game warden is the best decision I've ever made." Ethan paused to capture her gaze, his eyebrows furrowing inquisitively before continuing. "Enough about me. I'm curious about what brought you to Maine. Jaret mentioned you were here taking part in an artist-in-residence program?"

Abbie's passion for her work shone in her eyes as she bobbed her head enthusiastically. "While I was recovering from the attack, I had a lot of time to think about what I wanted to do with my life. I was offered the chance to spend three months in the Maine wilderness to focus on my photography, and I knew God had opened a door. It's an amazing opportunity. I'm using the time to launch my new career as a freelance nature photographer. I was just beginning to piece back all the fragments of my life. Now, Vince and his father want to destroy the peace I've found."

"I want you to know I'm not going to rest until I stop the Romola family from wreaking havoc with your life."

"I appreciate that. But I meant what I said when I told you I want to be a part of this, Ethan. I'm not going to sit on the sidelines while you take all the risks."

"Fair enough. That doesn't mean I'm going to allow you to put yourself in harm's way. We need to proceed with caution, considering who we're dealing with here. Got it?"

"Understood. So, what's the plan?"

"After breakfast tomorrow, we'll head for the chalet the Warden Service maintains in the mountains. My friend Jaret will meet us there. Originally, the intent was for him to fly you to the NYPD's safe house solo once the weather clears. Now that we know the threat is real, there's no way I'm letting him carry out this mission alone. Jaret is an exemplary detective. I trust him implicitly. Still, it would be foolhardy to underestimate what the Romolas are capable of. I intend to back him up."

Abbie's lips parted, but before she could utter a word, Caleb and Sarah arrived with dessert and coffee.

"Dinner was amazing," Abbie told their genial host and hostess.

Beaming, Sarah set a luscious-looking chocolate torte on the table. "I'm glad you enjoyed it. I hope you saved room for dessert."

"I'm stuffed, but you can bet I'm going to make room for that masterpiece of chocolate decadence." Abbie smiled.

Sarah grinned broadly. "I like her already, Ethan."

"Me, too," Caleb agreed with an approving smile.

Sarah cut a thick slice of the elegantly glazed torte. Setting it on a plate, she garnished it lavishly with whipped cream. "Ethan told us what the Romola family has put you through," she murmured sympathetically as she passed the dessert to Abbie. "I'm so sorry you had to endure all that. You're in the best of hands now, though."

"Do you have any idea why the Romolas are targeting you?" Caleb asked.

"Well, I didn't win any points with Vince Romola when I tried to investigate his less-than-scrupulous business dealings. But I don't think that's behind the Romola family's renewed interest in me."

"Is it possible the Romolas think you've continued looking into their dealings independently, and they're worried you might have dug up something that would be damaging to their business?" Caleb ventured.

Abbie frowned. "I don't know. I thought Vince was satisfied he'd crushed my spirit after he had me blacklisted. I gave up trying to unearth evidence I could use to prove his corrupt dealings after that. Even if I had wanted to continue my fact-finding mission, I was too focused on recovering from the injuries I sustained when Vito attacked me to have the time or energy to try."

"That's completely understandable," Caleb sympathized.

"I suppose the Romolas could blame me for Vito's death," Abbie speculated, racking her brain for other possible motives for their ruthless pursuit of her. "Vito might still be alive today if he hadn't abducted me that night and gotten caught in the act."

Ethan shook his head. "I don't think that's it, either. Vito was in my custody when the shooter took him out. If Edgar and Vince blame anyone for the Vito's death, it would be me. Besides, sad as it is to say, Edgar was totally unaffected by Vito's passing. While his son was alive, he treated him like an outcast. He hated that Vito never stepped up to work alongside him and Vince in the family business. And it's no secret that Vince and Vito were never close."

Sarah shook her head. "So, we're back to square one. We still have no idea what prompted the Romola family's renewed interest in Abbie."

"Don't worry. We'll piece this together," Caleb asserted. "We can talk things over more over breakfast tomorrow morning. Everything will be clearer after a good night's sleep."

While Caleb and Sarah returned to work to prepare the restaurant for the next day's business, Ethan and Abbie finished their dessert and headed back to the house to get some rest.

Escorting her upstairs, Ethan paused outside her door as they parted at their respective bedrooms. “Good night.”

Abbie returned his smile. “Good night.”

He watched until the door closed behind her, listening until he heard the click of the lock engaging. Considering the intense day she’d endured, she would probably fall asleep as soon as her head touched the pillow.

Satisfied she was safe, he headed for his room. He was exhausted, too, but he was too keyed up to rest. His mind was racing with unanswered questions.

Deciding a walk would clear his head, he collected Zane for a bit of exercise. It was still raining, but the German shepherd was a water dog through and through—he was totally unfazed by the wet weather and excited to burn off some energy, and the exercise helped Ethan let go of some of the tension from the last twenty-four hours.

Returning to the house, he fed his canine partner and then settled him down for the night outside Abbie’s room. With Zane on guard, he could at least try to get a few hours of shut-eye.

Entering his bedroom, he walked to the window. The lights were still on in the restaurant, but the number of cars and trucks in the parking lot had dwindled considerably. The remaining vehicles most likely belonged to guests who would be staying the night at the inn.

He was turning away from the window when he caught a flash of movement in the lot below. Spinning back around, he scanned the parking area and spotted a lanky man, his face concealed by the dark hoodie he wore, crouched down by a truck that was similar in make and model to Ethan's unmarked Warden Service vehicle. As he watched, the man rose slightly until he was even with the truck's driver's-side window and shined a penlight in the interior of the truck.

Ethan's eyes narrowed. Whatever the guy was up to, his actions had *no good* stamped all over them. There was a very good chance he was a member of the Romola crime family sent to search for Abbie. If he was, apprehending him could be a first step to getting the answers they so desperately needed.

Exiting his room, Ethan moved soundlessly down the hall. He was reassured by the sight of Zane in full guard mode outside Abbie's door. On the slim chance anyone was to elude Caleb's top-notch home security system, they wouldn't get past Zane.

Careful to move silently so he wouldn't wake Abbie, he hurried down the stairs and out into the dimly lit parking area. Halfway across the lot, he realized he'd left his Glock behind in his haste to catch up with the intruder. He'd have to count on the element of surprise.

He spotted Mr. Hoodie weaving his way sneakily around the vehicles in the lot. Stopping at the driver's-side door of another late-model truck that matched the make and model of his Warden Service vehicle, the man set to work trying to bypass the alarm.

Ethan picked up his pace, heading for the shadowy figure. "Stop right there," he commanded.

The man's head snapped up at the same time his hand dropped to his side. Drawing a gun, he leveled it at Ethan's chest and pulled the trigger.

FIVE

Propelled by the punch of danger-induced adrenaline surging through his veins, Ethan dived for the cover of the nearest vehicle. Fearing the evasive maneuver was too little, too late, he was shocked when he heard the soft click of an impotent trigger pull cut through the tense silence instead of the earsplitting crack of a round exiting the chamber.

Risking a glance around the bumper he'd taken shelter behind, he saw Mr. Hoodie fumbling with his pistol. His firearm had jammed!

Seizing the miraculous reprieve, Ethan launched himself at his attacker before his assailant could clear the malfunction. Tackling him to the ground, he wrestled the gun from his hand.

Enraged, Mr. Hoodie lashed out. With a strength belied by his slight build, the man fought wildly to reclaim the weapon. Busy blocking the onslaught of blows, Ethan wasn't aware that Caleb had rushed to the scene until he heard him bark out a command.

"Hands in the air," his friend ordered the hooded man, leveling his gun at the trespasser.

Glancing frantically around for a way out that wasn't

there, the man dropped his shoulders in defeat and raised his hands.

"Smart move," Ethan snapped, striding over to haul the suspect to his feet.

"I called 911," Caleb relayed as the urgent wail of sirens rose above the gusting gale. "I left the dogs to guard Sarah and Abbie. I'll text Sarah to let her know the situation is under control."

Two police cruisers sped into the parking lot, their strobing blue lights piercing the darkness. "Simmer down," Ethan warned the perp writhing in his grasp. "Don't make this situation any worse for yourself than it already is."

Stilling, Mr. Hoodie lowered his head. "I don't want any trouble."

Ethan glared at him. "You should have thought about that before you tried to shoot me. Fortunately for you, we're more concerned about the man you're working for. If you tell us where we can find Edgar Romola, we'll do our best to ensure the judge takes your cooperation into account."

Mr. Hoodie's eyes widened, the confusion streaking across his face obviously genuine. "I don't know no Romola," he stammered. "Trey Stapinski hired me. He said this gig would be a piece of cake. Said all I had to do was steal a truck that matched the specs he gave me and he'd pay me five grand. Should have known it wouldn't be that easy."

Caleb's eyebrows shot up. "Trey Stapinski is back at it again, huh? I thought he'd stay on the straight and narrow after being granted early release from prison, but I guess doing time for grand theft auto didn't teach him anything. Your bad judgment in getting involved with him has landed you in serious trouble. Trouble you only compounded when you tried to kill a law enforcement officer."

The responding policemen approached and took over. While one team escorted Mr. Hoodie to the police station, the other pair asked Ethan and Caleb to have a seat in the back of their cruiser, out of the storm, so they could take their statements.

After fielding the officers' questions, Ethan and Caleb returned to the house. The moment they walked through the door, Sarah and Abbie rushed up with Zane and Lucas at their sides.

Ethan's heart seized when he saw the concern darkening Abbie's eyes. Her beautiful features were shadowed with apprehension. He wanted nothing more than to erase the horror of the day and vaporize her worries.

"Thank God you're both okay," Abbie blurted.

"We were so worried!" Sarah added, hugging Caleb.

"We're fine." Caleb and Ethan uttered the assurance in unison.

"So, it was a random crime, unconnected to the men pursuing Abbie?" Sarah asked as the men removed their drenched jackets and hung them on the coatrack in the entryway.

"Yeah." Ethan nodded. "A car thief decided your parking lot would be a great place to fill his hot-wheels shopping list."

"Bad decision on his part," Caleb drawled. "An even worse decision to try and shoot his way out."

Abbie's appalled gaze bounced to Ethan. "He shot at you?"

Ethan shrugged off her concern. "He tried to. His gun

malfunctioned. Caleb came along at exactly the right moment and we were able to apprehend him."

"That was quite enough excitement for me for one night," Caleb chuckled. "Hopefully the rest of the evening will be uneventful."

"Amen to that," Ethan seconded.

Caleb concurred with a nod. "If you two are all set, Sarah and I are going to get some sleep. We'll see you at breakfast."

"Of course," Ethan assured him.

Watching Caleb and Sarah head to their room with Lucas, Abbie blinked sleepily. "It's bedtime, take two, for me."

Accompanying her upstairs, Ethan saw her safely to her room. Stopping in the hallway, he turned to her. "Zane will keep watch, and I'll be right next door, too," he assured her.

She smiled wearily. "Thank you. As disconcerting as it is to be targeted by the Romola family again, I'm glad you're in my corner."

Zane woofed softly, his massive head cocked to one side, and his intelligent eyes locked on hers questioningly as though he was wondering why she'd failed to mention him. "You, too, Zane," Abbie chuckled.

Ethan waited until Abbie was safely in her room before stepping into his. As he unpacked his bag, scenes from the parking lot encounter played in his mind like a surveillance feed stuck on loop. He'd narrowly avoided disaster tonight. He'd made a huge error in judgment when he'd gone after the intruder unarmed. His rash decision to confront the man when he didn't have his weapon with him could easily have resulted in a far different ending.

He was here to safeguard Abbie. He couldn't afford to make any more mistakes. Praying for the wisdom and guidance he would need as he strove to protect her and find the evidence necessary to prove the Romola family's wrongdoings, he thanked God for His faithfulness in seeing him through yet another dicey situation and for keeping Abbie safe from the men who were trying to harm her.

He added a prayer of gratitude for the blessing of Abbie's forgiveness after the way he'd checked out of her life without a backward glance. He didn't deserve the grace she'd shown him, but he would make the most of the free pass she'd given him. And, in turn, he would rectify the mistakes he'd made.

Closing his eyes for a second against the painful flood of memories, he turned his focus to the questions that continued to volley around his brain. The sooner he could puzzle out the Romola family's motive for targeting Abbie, the sooner he could put an end to the threat.

He was fully aware of how badly she wanted to get back to the work she loved. He intended to make that happen just as quickly as he could, but to do so he needed to put his hands on hard evidence that would prove the Romola family's wrongdoings.

Abbie woke the next morning to the drumming of rain against her bedroom window. The last thing she remembered was returning to her room after Ethan and Caleb had ended the scary situation that had unfolded after dinner. She'd been so exhausted she must have fallen asleep almost immediately after she'd gone to bed.

Last night, waiting for confirmation that Ethan was okay had been the longest half hour of her life. The relief that had washed over her when he'd walked through the door had been so intense it had made her heart ache.

She wasn't about to psychoanalyze her reaction. She was afraid of what doing a deep dive into her emotions might reveal. She couldn't let herself get attached to Ethan. He hadn't even wanted a place in her life as a friend—it was a waste of time to think he could be a part of her life as anything more.

Putting those disconcerting thoughts out of her head, she scrambled out of bed. She instantly regretted the too-swift movement when the still-healing tendons in her left leg tensed in protest. Gingerly making her way through her morning stretching routine, she relaxed as the exercise eased the stiffness in her muscles.

She ended her workout ready to face the day, whatever it might bring. She wasn't going to let Vince's resurrected vendetta stop her from rebuilding the life he'd so ruthlessly pillaged.

When she'd seen him in the woods yesterday, her initial instinct had been to tuck tail and run. It was a knee-jerk reaction to everything he and his twin brother had put her through. Maybe having Ethan here had jump-started her former boldness or maybe she was just tired of being beaten down, but, whatever the reason, she wasn't cowering in fear any longer. She was proud of that progress. She intended to continue on that path.

Fueled by her resolve, she armored up for the day in her favorite jeans, a purple silk shirt and ankle boots. The first round of the storm front had passed, and the rain had stopped for now. Newly gathering clouds affirmed the weather forecast calling for a second round of bad weather was on point.

Stepping out into the hall, she looked for Zane. The sweet-tempered German shepherd wasn't outside her door. Ethan must have taken him out for a walk.

Her assumption was confirmed when her knock on Ethan's door went unanswered. Following the enticing aroma of bacon, eggs and freshly brewed coffee, she made her way down to the kitchen.

Hearing her enter the room, Sarah glanced up from the batch of cinnamon rolls she was icing. "Good morning. You're just in time for breakfast. You look like you slept well, despite yesterday's scare."

Abbie returned the woman's warm smile. "Good morning. I slept like a baby, thanks. I'm sorry about all the chaos last night."

"You have nothing to apologize for. What happened wasn't your fault."

Abbie worried her bottom lip. "I was afraid I'd brought trouble to your door."

"You didn't. Even if you had, we would have dealt with it. I think Caleb is secretly hoping he'll have a chance to go head to head with the Romola family. He'll never admit it, but he sometimes misses the thrill of detective work."

"You've built something really special together. It's obvious you both enjoy running the restaurant and inn."

Sarah's blue eyes sparkled. "We do! This is going to sound corny, but this is our dream come true. Selfishly, I'm relieved Caleb chose this as his retirement sideline instead of working as a private detective or in some other law enforcement–related job."

Grabbing two mugs and the pot of coffee, Sarah set them down on the table before nodding toward the breakfast spread laid out on the kitchen island. "Go ahead and fix a plate and have a seat. The guys are out walking the dogs before the next storm front moves in. Knowing how those two get lost in shop talk when they're with each other, they'll be a while."

Her appetite sparked by the delicious smells suffusing the cozy kitchen, Abbie didn't need to be told twice. Filling a mug with coffee and adding sugar and a generous amount of cream to the fragrant brew, she took a grateful sip. "Delicious," she sighed.

"Caleb roasts his own special blend of beans for the restaurant. Now I'm spoiled for anything else."

Breaking off a flaky chunk of warm cinnamon roll, Abbie popped it in her mouth. "Amazing!" She groaned in blissful appreciation as the flavors of brown sugar, cinnamon and sweet icing exploded on her tongue. "You and Caleb make the perfect team. You're both talented cooks and wonderful hosts."

"We love sharing our little piece of paradise with visitors. When this all blows over, I hope you and Ethan will come back for a longer stay."

"I'll definitely be back. I'm sure Ethan will be, too."

"Together, I hope. Caleb and I aren't the only ones who make a great team. You and Ethan complement each other perfectly."

"Oh, it's not like that," Abbie quickly dismissed. "Ethan is only here with me because he has to be. There's nothing personal between us."

Sarah regarded her thoughtfully. "I've known Ethan a long time. If you ask me, there's more at play here than just his professional obligations. The way he looks at you speaks volumes. I can tell he cares about you."

Sarah's words triggered a pang of longing. Abbie

wished the woman's observation was true. "I never would have made it back from the dark place I was in after the attack if not for his unwavering support. Ethan cares about me in the way he cares about all the people he's entrusted to protect. He's compassionate and kind, and he brings those attributes to his work."

"That's the Ethan I know," Sarah agreed. "May I speak freely?"

"Of course."

"The whole precinct was shocked when Ethan resigned. He lived and breathed the job. He insisted he was just looking for a change of pace, but Caleb and I know him well. Though he wouldn't acknowledge it, we think there was more to the story than what he was willing to share. In Ethan's mind, he'd failed both you and his partner. I think that misplaced belief propelled him toward a new career path where he felt there would be less risk of letting anyone else down."

Abbie's eyebrows rose. "But he's not responsible for what happened to me. He saved my life!"

Sarah nodded. "You and I know that, but Ethan is a complicated soul. He lost both of his parents at a young age. His uncle raised him. Nothing Ethan did was ever good enough to earn his uncle's approval, but that didn't stop him from trying to attain it. The man did a number on him—he never gave Ethan the acceptance he was seeking. Ethan is incredibly hard on himself as a result. I think it's why he always holds the people he cares about at arm's length. Like he does you."

Abbie didn't know what to say to that. Ethan hadn't even been interested in staying in touch with her, so she wasn't on his radar in *that* way. Of course, she didn't blame him for that. The wounds Vito had inflicted were enough to ensure no man would ever see her as desirable. She would carry the cross-hatching of knife tracks that marred her left leg from thigh to knee for the rest of her life. The chiseled etchings of ragged scars made her damaged goods.

In the highly unlikely event Ethan ever were to come to care for her, she couldn't count on him to stay. No one she cared about ever did. The man who'd fathered her hadn't stuck around long enough to know she even existed. Her mother had signed her over to strangers before becoming a casualty of the drug addiction that held her captive. She'd spent her childhood being bounced from foster home to foster home. Why would Ethan be any different than anyone else in her life?

Needing to veer the conversation away to a topic that wouldn't tempt her to mistake Ethan's sense of duty for something more personal, she deftly switched gears. "Now it's my turn to ask for permission to speak freely."

"By all means."

"Caleb mentioned you were targeted by a stalker. If you don't mind my asking, I'm curious how long it took before you felt like you were beginning to get past what happened to you. I'm trying to move on from the Slayer's attack, but I'm frustrated by the amount of time it's taking me to feel normal again and how the most insignificant things have a way of bringing the horror flooding back. I'm working hard to bury the awful memories of that night, but they still crop up when I least expect them to. Does it ever get any easier?"

Reaching for her hand, Sarah gave it an encouraging squeeze. "I can tell you with one hundred percent certainty that it does. You'll need to be patient, though. You can't expect to recover from the nightmare you went through in just a few months. It's going to take a while. I was blessed—Ethan happened along before things escalated. It was a terrifying experience, but it could have been far worse. I can tell you with confidence that time does help. So does prayer, along with the support of people you care about."

"I'm impatient for things to get back to the way they were before the attack. And just when I thought I might be done with having to look over my shoulder, I'm having to deal with the Romolas again. I just want all this to be over."

Sarah clucked softly in understanding. "Of course you do. You have every right to want your life to return to normal. I remember feeling the same impatience and frustration. What helped me the most was reminding myself that no matter how bad the circumstances might seem at the moment, God has a plan. Trust in that. It will help you get through this trial."

"I worry that I might have brought this on myself somehow."

"I can relate to that. After Ethan apprehended the man who was stalking me, I kept replaying all the events of the weeks leading up to the incident. I was sure I must have somehow done something to provoke him. I believed I was responsible for what happened because I'd unknowingly made myself a target. Once I let go of that ridiculous notion, I started to heal. Never once think you're to blame for what Vito Romola did to you. Trials like what you and I went through, and like the trial you're faced with now, are 'let go and let God' moments."

Abbie felt a weight lift from her shoulders as she soaked in the wisdom of Sarah's words. "Thank you," she murmured gratefully.

Sarah drew her in for a hug. "Remember, I'm just a phone call away anytime you need someone to talk to."

Topping off her coffee cup, Abbie contemplated what Sarah had shared about Ethan's tendency to hold the people he cared about at arm's length. She wanted, more than anything, to believe the reason he'd distanced himself from her was due to that propensity. She wanted to view his reappearance in her life as a second chance to forge a friendship with him. But he didn't want her friendship. He'd made that plain when he'd left New York without even saying goodbye.

It would take more than Ethan's unannounced and hasty departure from her life for her to evict him from the special place he occupied in her heart, but she knew better than to set herself up for another letdown by allowing herself to hope he'd come looking for her because she meant something to him. She'd do well to remember she was only an assignment to him. He was here because there was work to be done and bad guys to be brought to justice. Thinking this unexpected reunion could lead to anything else would only end in disappointment.

SIX

It was almost noon when Abbie and Ethan said goodbye to Caleb and Sarah and set out on the drive to the Maine Warden Service's chalet. As the miles sped by, the only noise to permeate the silence was the occasional soft snore from the napping Zane and the rhythmic swishing of the wipers working double-time to keep the windshield clear of the heavy rain that had begun falling again shortly after they'd left the inn.

Ethan was uncharacteristically quiet, and the tense set of his jaw and the stranglehold he had on the steering wheel told Abbie something weightier than the ferocious intensity of round two of the storm was worrying him. Whatever it was, she wasn't going to let him carry the weight of the burden he was dealing with alone.

"Want to talk about it?" she prompted gently.

He sent her an apologetic smile before turning his attention back to the road. "Sorry. I'm not very good company today, am I? It's just that I keep running the events of the past twenty-four hours through my head, and I can't shake the feeling I'm missing something."

Opting for a glass-half-full approach, she pointed out the only bright spot in this whole mess that she could think of other than having Ethan here by her side. "At least we've lost the goons Vince sicced on us."

Ethan's doubtful expression told her he didn't share her optimism. "I'm not so sure of that. I'm not going to make the mistake of underestimating the Romola family. I reached out to Jaret last night to loop him in on the break-in at your cabin. Afterward, he contacted the owner of the property to see if the cabin might have a surveillance camera he could get footage from. That was a dead end, but it turns out the owner doesn't live far from the place and he drove out to check on things. He called Jaret when he got back to tell him he'd found a cuff link in the driveway. It was monogrammed with the letter *R*."

Abbie's eyes widened. "That's great! Jaret can get prints or DNA evidence from it, right?"

Ethan's lips tightened in a grim line. "Unfortunately, no. The cuff link was half-buried in mud and exposed to the elements, and the owner of the cabin handled it before it could be properly processed. Any potential evidence was either contaminated or lost entirely. Still, the cuff link is enough to confirm what you and I already know."

"Vince Romola was there," she pronounced, echoing his certainty. "What I still don't understand is why. I dropped my investigation months ago. If he wants me out of the way permanently, why did he wait so long?"

"His renewed interest in you has to be related to something that's only recently come to his attention. Is it possible he thinks you're still pursuing your investigation, even though you're no longer working as a photojournalist?"

"I suppose that's one likelihood. If that's what he believes, he's wrong. No news agency or media outlet will give me the time of day after he saw to it that I was blacklisted, so even if I did find evidence to prove what he's wrapped up in, I'd have a difficult time proving the info is credible." Cocking her head, Abbie regarded him thoughtfully. "Maybe this is all just a matter of Vince picking back up his vendetta against me for my earlier attempt at exposing him."

Ethan's lips dipped in a contemplative frown. "It's plausible this is about settling a personal score, but it's not probable. The way your cabin was ransacked indicates Vince and his associates were looking for something they're convinced you have."

Abbie exhaled a frustrated breath. "I just want this nightmare to be over so I can get back to focusing on my freelance photography. Three months of creative immersion in the Maine wilderness is a gift when it comes to getting my new career off the ground. Every day I lose is a day I'll never get back. Vince torpedoed my photojournalism career. I'm not going to let him and his father rob me of this chance to make a fresh start without a fight."

"I get where you're coming from, but you've seen how dangerous the Romolas are. They're experts at evading the law, and they aren't afraid to do whatever it takes to get what they want. Right now, what they want is you."

"I'm not scared of them."

"I know you aren't, and I admire your courage. But they're scared of *you*. That makes them dangerously unpredictable. Edgar and his associates have taken some big risks pursuing you so boldly. Whatever it is they're after, it's something important enough that they're willing to put everything on the line for it. If we can figure out what they're so desperate to get their hands on, that might give us a clue as to what this is all about."

"But I don't know anything. I didn't collect any tangible evidence when I was digging around for proof of Vince's illicit dealings, and I never got far enough into the investigation to delve into Edgar's involvement in the shady parts of the Romola family business. I was too focused on Vince."

"Even if you had looked into Edgar, it's unlikely you would have turned up anything useful. Law enforcement has yet to prove his connection to anything criminal, even though he's up to his neck in dirty dealings."

"Vito was the only Romola family member who slipped up and got caught. And he's dead now."

Ethan nodded gravely. "The blame for that rests squarely on my shoulders. Vito killed my partner. I was so focused on getting revenge for Gabriella's death the night I apprehended him that I dropped my guard. If Vito hadn't been murdered while he was in my custody, there's no question he would have been convicted of the dozens of murders he committed as the Spitting Image Slayer. And he might have shared information that could have been invaluable in building a case against Vince and Edgar."

"You're not responsible," Abbie asserted. "You had no way of knowing someone was going to shoot Vito that night. Besides, what if the person who killed him wasn't trying to extract their own brand of justice? What if they wanted to silence him before he could stand trial? I wonder if Vito might have been holding something over his father's head in an attempt to blackmail him. If so, Edgar could be behind his death."

Ethan whistled. "I've bounced Vito's murder against every possible scenario I could think of, but I never contemplated the likelihood his father might have had a hand in it. That's a solid theory. You should think about becoming a detective."

Abbie chuckled. "I'll stick with photography, thanks. I'd rather shoot photos than get shot at."

"There's wisdom in that," Ethan drawled, amusement swirling in the depths of his blue eyes before his expression shifted to one of intense resolve. "I promise I'm going to do everything in my power to get you back to the work you love as soon as possible. We'll meet Jaret at the Maine Warden Service's chalet today, and we'll stay there overnight. By tomorrow morning, the front that's fueling this string of storms should have moved out. As soon as the skies are clear enough to get a helicopter up, we'll head to the safe house in New York. We'll spend a few days there lying low while Jaret's team works to gather enough evidence to put the Romola family behind bars."

Abbie wanted to protest his strategy. She didn't want to run and hide. She wanted to dig in her heels and go head to head with the Romolas. But Ethan wasn't a coward. He didn't back down from danger. If he was on board with this plan, it was for a very good reason. He was a seasoned law enforcement officer. If he thought putting some distance between her and the Romola family was the smart thing to do, then she'd abide by his call.

"Okay," she conceded. "But I'm not going to waste the next few days sitting around doing nothing. I have my laptop with me. I plan on going back over the information I gathered when I was looking into Vince Romola's business dealings to see if I might have overlooked something."

Ethan nodded his approval. "While you pursue that angle, Jaret and I will do a deep dive into all the intel the

NYPD has gathered. Up to this point, the taskforce working the case have come up dry when it comes to finding proof of the Romolas' criminal dealings that will stand up in court. The cuff link isn't admissible as evidence, but it's proof we're on the right track."

The conviction lacing Ethan's words and the certainty that things were moving in the right direction filled Abbie with hope. "We should also look into Edgar's possible connection to Vito's murder."

Ethan nodded. "I agree. There are plenty of people who would say Vito got what he had coming. As badly as I wanted him to pay for what he did to my partner, I never wanted things to end for him the way they did. If he'd been brought to trial, justice would have been served and the families of his victims would have had a greater peace."

Steeling herself against the wave of grief that crashed over her at the memory of the innocent lives lost, Abbie swallowed back the lump of emotion clogging her throat. "I keep thinking about Leanne Renton, the other woman Vito abducted the night he captured me. He only took her because he needed someone who looked like me to complete his twisted spitting-image ritual. It tears me apart to think that she'd be alive today if she hadn't resembled me."

Ethan's eyes softened, brimming with empathy. "Don't torture yourself. If Vito hadn't chosen her, he would have gone after someone else who looked like you. If we're going to play the what-if game, things could have ended differently if I'd only acted sooner when I got the call with the tip that the Spitting Image Slayer was gearing up to commit another double murder. The last thing I wanted to do was drag anyone else into another ambush like the one I'd lost Gabriella to, so I made the decision to go after him alone. I lost valuable time gearing up for a solo response. If I'd gotten there sooner, I might have been able to stop Vito before he had a chance to abduct you and Leanne. She'd still be alive, and I would have ended his rampage before he had a chance to hurt you."

Abbie fervently wished things would have played out that way. Leanne's death was heart-wrenchingly senseless, but Ethan had done everything in his power to prevent the tragedy. He'd acted single-handedly and taken on a knife-wielding maniac with zero hesitation. He'd stopped Vito from plunging his blade through her heart. If Ethan hadn't shown up when he did…

She wouldn't dwell on that now. Couldn't. The memories were still too raw and painful. "I owe my life to you—and not only because you saved me from a serial killer. You're the reason I didn't give up in my darkest moments after the attack."

Rubbing the back of his neck, Ethan let out a breath. "I could say the same thing about you, you know."

Abbie's forehead wrinkled in puzzlement. "Me? I don't see how. I relied on you, but I never offered you anything in return. The entire time I was recovering in the hospital, I was too busy leaning on you for support to pour anything into your life."

"That's where you're wrong. You saved me from myself. Emotionally, I was in a pretty bad place when I rescued you. I'd decided to give up my badge. I couldn't continue working in law enforcement when the mistakes I'd made had such catastrophic and irreversible consequences."

Abbie cringed, mortified by the realization that she'd failed to see the personal challenge Ethan had been navigating. "I'm so sorry. I can't believe I was so wrapped up in what I was going through that I didn't realize you were going through a tough time, too."

"Every time I visited you during your recovery, I always left inspired by your grit and tenacity. Your life had been turned upside down not once but twice, yet you continued to soldier on. Even after all you'd been through, you still maintained a positive attitude. If you weren't quitting, then how could I? You made me rethink my decision to give up law enforcement completely. You're the reason I looked for an alternative way to serve and protect rather than walking away from the work I love."

Abbie's heart broke for the burden he'd carried so unnecessarily. "I wish you'd told me what you were going through."

"You were facing your own challenges. I didn't want to add to them."

"But I would have wanted to help. That's what friends are for." She paused, struggling to express the hurt that had weighed down her heart for so long—hurt she hadn't wanted to acknowledge but could no longer ignore. "Only, you didn't want me to be a part of your life in that way, did you?"

Ethan's lips compressed in a firm line. "Friendship is a liability in my line of work. If you'd remained a part of my life, sooner or later things would have become complicated. I didn't want to hurt you."

"I just wish you would have told me how you felt instead of just disappearing. I never even had a chance to say goodbye."

"I know, and I'm sorry for that. The depravity I was seeing as a detective was poisoning my soul. I had to leave the NYPD. If I'd stayed on, I would have lost a huge part of myself. When the position with the Maine Warden Service opened up, things happened fast. There wasn't time for goodbyes. The move to Maine has been good for me. Trading in my NYPD badge to work as a game warden has given me a measure of peace."

"I'm glad you've found where you belong."

"And I'm happy you're building a new life doing what you love. I promise you I'm going to put an end to the Romola family's terror tactics so you can go back to that life without constantly having to look over your shoulder."

At the reminder of the reason why she was being forced to be hyperaware, Abbie's smile of gratitude faltered. "I want to trust that everything is going to be okay, but I have to confess the *why me*s I let smother my faith after the attack have crept back. I wish my conviction was stronger."

"Trust me, I've done my fair share of asking *why me?* Experiencing doubt from time to time doesn't mean our faith is weak. It means we're human. Does life sometimes throw us devastating curveballs that make us wonder why a loving God would allow such horrific things to occur? Sure. But when catastrophes occur, we just have to remind ourselves there's a reason God allowed them to touch our lives."

"You make it sound so easy."

"It's anything but easy. I find it helps if I replace the *why me*s with *even if*s. Like in this situation you're facing, even if the Romola family continues to target you,

God is in control of the situation. He's got this. He won't let any harm come to you. Neither will I."

Ethan reached out to take her hand, squeezing it gently in reassurance. Her breath caught in her throat, her heart giving a hopeful leap at the intensity of the feelings the contact sparked.

She quickly reminded herself she had no business reading anything into the gesture. Even if there was a possibility they could be friends, Ethan had made it abundantly clear that friendship could never grow to anything more.

She needed to learn to be grateful for whatever part he was willing to play in her life. He was here with her, now, and together they would end the Romola family's rampage. Then she'd move on with her life. And if the knowledge that doing so would mean moving on without Ethan as a permanent part of that life stung more than it should, she'd simply have to get over it—and him.

Realizing his fingers were still enfolded around Abbie's, Ethan froze. What was he doing? Reminding himself of his vow to keep their relationship purely professional, he quickly drew his hand away.

A vicious gust of wind swept his truck, making him glad both his hands were firmly back on the wheel. The storm was showing no sign of letting up. The rain pelted the truck, and the wind was whipping over the mountaintop in a ferocious onslaught that had the pine trees lining the roadway bending under the force of the blustery gale.

As they drove further, the route's gradual ascent suddenly turned steeper. The deeper they traveled into the wilderness, the denser the tree cover grew. A few miles later, the pavement transitioned to dirt, narrowing to a single lane.

Abbie turned to him, concern filling her captivating green eyes. “We’re not lost, are we?”

Ethan chuckled. “I realize it seems like we’re about to be swallowed up by a pine forest, but we’re headed in the right direction. The chalet is tucked in the middle of this mountain range. The Warden Service uses the property for training exercises and team-building retreats. It’s off the beaten path, but that’s exactly what we need at the moment. The property also has a helicopter pad and a chopper on-site for search and rescue operations. We’ll use the helicopter to take you to the NYPD safe house as soon as the weather allows.”

“There’ll be a pilot at the chalet, then?”

“You’re looking at him.”

“You fly?”

“Yup. I’m full of surprises.” He winked. “Actually, Jaret is a licensed pilot, too. Since I’ve invited myself along, I figure I might as well make myself useful.”

Ethan found himself on the receiving end of a look of mock concern from Abbie. “I don’t know how I feel about that. Who’s the better pilot?”

“That would be me, of course,” he replied with an unabashed grin.

As they rounded the next bend in the road, a gorgeous chalet came into view. Wood smoke billowed from the stone chimney, indicating a cozy fire had been set to ward off the rainstorm’s chill.

“We’re here,” he announced, pulling up under the chalet’s carport. “Looks like Jaret beat us. I gave him the code for the security system in case he made better time on the road. Knowing him, he's already made himself at home in the kitchen. Back when we worked together, we used to take turns cooking meals for the team when we pulled the holiday shifts."

"I'm guessing Jaret is the better chef?" Abbie ventured teasingly.

Ethan's reply was preceded by an amused eye roll. "First you disparage my flying skills. Now you're trash talking my abilities in the kitchen? What, one shot at my ego wasn't enough?"

Still chuckling at their lighthearted banter, Abbie exited the truck as a tall, athletically built man with blond hair and arresting green eyes stepped out of the chalet to welcome them.

"Ethan. Glad you made it safely." The man smiled before turning his attention—along with a megadose of charm—to Abbie. "And you must be the woman I've heard so much about."

"Jaret, meet Abbie. Abbie, this is Jaret," Ethan introduced.

"It's great to meet you, Abbie. I'm just finishing up preparing dinner, so go on in and make yourself at home. I'll help Ethan get your bags inside."

"Thanks," Abbie replied, returning his warm smile.

Moving to the back door of the truck, Ethan let Zane out. As soon as the K-9's paws hit the ground, he made a beeline for Jaret, greeting him with the same enthusiasm he showed for his favorite dog treats.

Dropping to one knee, Jaret rubbed the dog's head affectionately. When the door to the chalet closed behind Abbie, he whistled softly. "How come you never told me she was so beautiful? And don't try and tell me you never noticed. There's no way I'm buying that."

"I noticed. Now, if you're done charming my K-9 and the woman we're here to protect, how about focusing on our mission?" Ethan tossed back lightly. At least he hoped the question came across as a teasing chastisement rather than the annoyed rebuke he was trying hard to suppress. "Anything new to report?"

Ruffling Zane's ears affectionately and giving him a final pat, Jaret rose to his feet. "That's a negative, pal. Unless we come across something that points us in a different direction, we're still operating on the theory that the Romola family believes Abbie has something in her possession with the power to expose them. We just need to decipher what that something is."

"And keep them from getting to her first," Ethan uttered gravely. "I hope you don't mind, but I'm inviting myself along when you take Abbie to the safe house. I know you can handle things, but considering who we're dealing with, you can't argue that extra reinforcements wouldn't be prudent."

"You're right," Jaret agreed. "And I meant what I told you when you agreed to help. If things should go sideways on this mission, there's no one I'd rather have at my six than you."

"Thanks, buddy. I'm going to take Zane for a short walk before I bring him inside."

"While you do that, I'll take care of the bags."

Ethan had only walked a short distance with his K-9 when the German shepherd froze. Ears perked, he tilted his head toward the tree line. Following his dog's gaze, his pulse kicked into overdrive as he spotted what had caught Zane's attention. Two beams of light were bobbing through the pines. 'No Trespassing' signs marked the property line, making it clear this was private land. There shouldn't be anyone out here, especially after dark. Poachers, perhaps? Or someone with something even more sinister in mind?

"Suke!" Ethan commanded softly, giving the K-9 permission to track down the trespassers. Turning his flashlight to a lower setting so as not to give their location away, Ethan followed Zane as he moved swiftly through the darkened forest, silently closing the distance.

Mere feet remained between them and the trespassers when their lights stilled. He automatically dropped his hand to his holster, preparing for trouble. A moment later, a masculine voice drifted his way.

"Look at all the tracks!" the man enthused. "Matt was right, there's prime hunting to be had here."

Ethan's jaw tightened as a wave of anger crashed over him. They *were* here to hunt illegally. Any other time, he'd cite them for trespassing and intent to poach, but he couldn't afford to lose sight of his mission. He was here to protect Abbie. As much as he hated to do it, he was going to have to let these two go.

"Good evening, gentlemen," he intoned authoritatively. He stepped into view, counting on his uniform and Zane growling menacingly at his side to communicate that they were in deep trouble.

Caught by surprise, the men simply gaped at him. Since it didn't appear they had anything to say for themselves, he decided to save them the trouble. "I don't know what you're doing out here, but given it's after dark, and you're armed and carrying spotlights, this doesn't look good for you. Hunting is prohibited in this area, as the signs clearly state. I'm sure you're both aware there are penalties for poaching."

The man closest to him shifted nervously from one booted foot to the other. "We haven't shot anything."

Ethan fixed him with a pointed stare. He was inclined to believe the man's claim. That didn't mean he was going to let them off the hook without making them squirm a bit. "Maybe not, but those rifles slung across your shoulders tell me you aren't out here to check out the constellations. I have other priorities tonight, so. I'm going to let you off with a warning. Now, get out of here, and don't even think about pulling a stunt like this again. If I catch you hunting illegally out here again, you'll be exchanging that camo for prison-orange jumpsuits."

The men couldn't leave fast enough. Mumbling their thanks, they hastily headed off. Ethan hated letting them go, but he hated even more the idea of anything happening to Abbie because he'd allowed a couple of men with bad intentions to fracture his focus.

Bending, he patted Zane. "Good job, boy. Let's head back to the chalet. There's a treat waiting there with your name on it."

After giving the dog dinner and one of his favorite dog biscuits as a reward for a job well-done, Ethan headed for the kitchen to join Jaret and Abbie.

"Glad you found your way back," Jaret teased. "I thought I was going to have to go and search for you. When you said you were taking Zane for a walk, I didn't realize you meant you were making it a marathon."

Ethan grinned wryly. "The walk turned eventful. Zane and I flushed out a couple of would-be poachers."

Jaret raised an eyebrow. "All okay now, I take it?"

Ethan nodded. "They won't be back."

"Good," Abbie declared firmly, her expression making her disdain for illegal hunting evident. "Where's Zane?"

"I fed him, and now he's sleeping off his meal in front of the fireplace."

Jaret moved to set the table. "Your dog is spoiled. Our dinner is ready. Let's eat so we can go and enjoy that fireplace after, too."

The feast of steamed lobster tails with seafood stuffing, roasted potatoes, coleslaw and rolls Jaret prepared was exceptional. After enjoying strawberry shortcake for dessert, the trio took their coffee mugs and moved to the large, cushy sectional in the great room.

Zane lifted his head to see what was going on when they entered the room, then promptly returned to his doggie dreams.

Watching the K-9 slumbering peacefully, Abbie's lips curved in a smile. "I hope I can sleep that soundly tonight."

Wanting nothing more than to allay her fears, Ethan smiled reassuringly. "You can rest easy. The Romolas won't come looking for you here. And just to be doubly safe, Jaret and I will take turns keeping watch tonight. Zane will, too, once he's caught up on his beauty sleep."

"Since the chalet is off the Romolas' radar, couldn't we just stay here? Why bother to travel to the NYPD's safe house?"

Jaret glanced at Ethan before answering. "Ethan and I discussed the possibility of using this chalet rather than the NYPD's safe house. While we're both confident there's no immediate risk of the Romola family looking for you here, another twenty-four hours could change that. It's best if we stick to the original plan."

Ethan nodded in agreement. "My truck is unmarked, but I was wearing my Warden Service uniform when we encountered the Romolas' cronies. There's a very good chance they'll start looking for real estate that's connected to the Warden Service to search for you. If they do, they could find us."

"That makes sense," Abbie agreed.

No sooner than she'd uttered the words, the lights flickered and went out, pitching the chalet into darkness save for the embers glowing in the fireplace.

Every nerve in his body tensing, Ethan shifted to high-alert mode. Had the Romolas somehow found them and sabotaged the power? If so, their time for figuring out what the crime family wanted from Abbie before a show-down ensued had just run out.

SEVEN

Roused by the commotion from the blackout, Zane sat up on his haunches and surveyed the room. Deciding there was nothing going on worth interrupting his nap for, the German shepherd promptly returned to making the most of his comfortable snoozing spot.

Seeing the K-9's lack of concern, Abbie exhaled a relieved breath. "Zane isn't worried. The storm must be responsible for the power outage, not the bad guys."

"Agreed," Jaret seconded, as the chalet's backup generator kicked in and the great room was once again bathed in cozy light. "If an intruder had cut the power, they would have disabled the generator, too."

Nodding, Abbie stifled a yawn. The combination of the delicious meal and the cozy fire had taken the edge off the adrenaline rush from the day's terrifying events, and now she was having a hard time keeping her eyes open.

Ethan stood and put another log on the fire. "We have a busy day ahead of us tomorrow. We should get some rest. Jaret and I will take turns standing guard. I'll take the first shift."

"Do you really need to keep watch?" Abbie asked. "No one knows we're here."

"True, but I'd rather not take any chances," Ethan replied.

Too exhausted to argue, Abbie wished the men goodnight and stopped to pat Zane on her way out of the room. Running her fingers through his silky coat was as calming as Ethan's reassuring strength and confidence. She giggled when the dog rewarded her with a sloppy kiss. She headed upstairs to bed with a lighter heart.

Abbie woke the next morning, surprised to find she'd slept well past her usual 6:00 a.m. rise-and-shine time. A glance out the window revealed yesterday's storm clouds had given way to sunshine.

After cleaning up, she donned a comfortable top and jeans and made her way downstairs. There, she found Ethan and Jaret sitting at the kitchen table sharing a platter of the biggest blueberry muffins she'd ever seen.

"I was wondering why you let me sleep so late," she teased. "Now it makes sense. You wanted to keep those pastry masterpieces all to yourselves."

Ethan's lips curved in a grin that made her pulse stutter. "You're on to us. Seriously, though, we fully intend to share. Jaret baked them, and they're amazing."

Jaret shrugged off the praise. "Thanks, but the credit goes to the fresh blueberries I picked up at the farm stand when I stopped to get supplies yesterday. There's a pot of coffee on the counter. Grab a cup and join us."

Abbie didn't need any prodding to indulge in a mug of the aromatic brew and one of the still-warm muffins. As she enjoyed her breakfast, Ethan and Jaret updated her on their plans for the day.

"The weather bureau says the storm front is pushing away slower than they'd forecasted," Jaret relayed. "There's a spot of clearing for a few hours, but there's more wind and rain on the way behind it. The conditions could be severe enough to make air travel treacherous. We'll have to wait until this afternoon to take the helicopter up."

Ethan rose to top off his coffee. His gaze homed in on hers when he returned to the table. "Since there's a break in the rain and we have a few hours to spare, would you like to take a walk and grab some pictures, Abbie? I know of a spot just a short hike from here where you can get some up-close and personal images of a family of foxes."

"That would be amazing."

"Great. It's a plan, then."

Jaret nodded. "I'll hang back and make sure the chopper is ready to go when the final remnants of the storm have passed by. You can leave Zane here with me so he doesn't interfere with Abbie's photos."

"Sounds good. Zane is infatuated with foxes, but they're not as enthusiastic about him. Isn't that right, buddy?"

The German shepherd barked his agreement, his tail thumping loudly against the floor at the mention of foxes.

After breakfast, Abbie set out with Ethan to explore the forest trails surrounding the chalet. The hike helped loosen the stiff muscles in her healing leg, and the rain-kissed, evergreen-scented air was a balm to her soul.

Reveling in the warm caress of the sun and the sights and sounds of nature, she said a prayer of thanks for this unexpected respite amid the uncertainty of her situation. Experiencing joy in moments like these was something she'd never take for granted again. Her heart had been so hollow in the weeks after the attack. With every waking moment tainted by memories of the nightmare she'd endured, she'd forgotten what happiness felt like. The terror had haunted her dreams, as well. And though the physical pain of her injuries was torture, the emotional agony of feeling like God had forsaken her had only multiplied the hurt a thousand times over.

She'd been on the brink of turning her back on Him, convinced He'd abandoned her when she needed Him the most, when Ethan had talked her off that ledge. She hated to think of what things would be like for her if he hadn't been there to pour faith back into her life and show her the way again. She owed him so much. And now, here he was giving her another amazing gift in this up-close and personal time with nature. And the gift of this time with him, too. Something, she reminded herself, she shouldn't get used to.

Looking up from adjusting her camera settings, her gaze tangled with Ethan's. Her breath hitched in her chest at the intensity of emotion in his piercing blue gaze as he smiled at her. Could the warmth swirling in the depths of his eyes indicate he was beginning to view spending time with her as more than just duty?

"We're almost there," he said, offering her a hand up the steep incline in front of them.

His strong hand gently wrapped around hers. She felt safe. Loved.

Get a grip, she mentally lectured herself, annoyed that she'd let her thoughts stray there. Her self-chastising moment didn't alter the fact that she felt bereft when he released her hand. Once again, she quickly tamped down the spark of hope his touch ignited. It was strictly a platonic gesture. He'd made it very clear there could never be anything between them.

Groaning inwardly at her foolishness, she reminded herself he was only here because he had a job to do. She had no business interpreting the comforting gesture as anything more than Ethan being his thoughtful self.

Emerging from the woods, they stepped out into a grassy field that seemed to stretch out forever. Ethan gestured toward a rocky outcropping a few yards ahead. "The fox den is right up there. The best seat in the house is behind that large rock to the left of us."

They quietly settled down behind the boulder. It wasn't long before a mother red fox, three young kits in tow, came into view. While the trio of adorable little fluff balls chased each other, cavorting through the meadow, their mother hunted for breakfast.

Being so close to these wild creatures was simply magical. Abbie captured image after image, totally captivated. The vixen was stunning, her red fur coat accented by her black legs, black-tipped ears and bushy, white-tipped tail. Every time Abbie's gaze connected with the wise, golden eyes of the mother fox through her camera lens, the beauty of the exchange took her breath away. Peace washed over her. She knew with one hundred percent certainty that *this* was what she was called to do. She was excited for the opportunity to share priceless moments like these with others through her images.

She was drawn from her musings when, with an impressive high jump, the vixen pounced on her quarry, catching her brunch. Rounding up her little family, the mother fox trotted off into the woods with her brood.

Abbie turned to Ethan. The expression on his face told

her he'd enjoyed the magical moment in time as much as she had. "Thank you," she enthused. "I got some amazing photos. An entire SD card's worth. I need to grab a new one."

Collecting her camera bag to swap the card she'd just filled with a blank one, she unzipped the pocket that contained her extra gear. Reaching for a replacement SD card, she paused, her hand hovering uncertainly over the bag. "Hmm. That's strange."

Seeing the color drain from Abbie's face and detecting the note of concern in her voice, Ethan instantly shifted to protector mode. "Everything okay?"

"There's a flash drive in my camera case along with my SD cards," she replied, her forehead furrowed, perplexed. "It's not mine."

"Are you sure?"

"Positive. I'm very picky about the brand I use. This one is by a different manufacturer than my go-to is. Plus, I never store my flash drives with my SD cards. Someone's definitely been in my bag. But who? Why? And how did they get to my case without me noticing?"

His pulse skittered. "When was the last time you accessed that compartment?"

"Other than just now, not since the night I was attacked. I put my camera equipment up after Vince had me ousted from the news agency. I'd only taken it back out the night Vito abducted me. I was doing a nocturnal photo shoot to capture some photos of owls when he grabbed me. I'm positive the flash drive wasn't in my case when I got my camera ready that night, so the flash drive had to have been placed there sometime after that. Since the case was stored in the bedroom closet of my apartment in New York until I came to Maine for the visiting artist program, that would have been tricky. And I'm sure I would have noticed if someone had broken into my apartment."

He inhaled sharply. According to Abbie's timeline, the most logical opportunity for someone to place the flash drive in her camera case would have been when Vito attacked her. Other than Abbie and Leanne, only he, Vito, and the first responders were there the night of the attack. Had Vito left it? If so, to what end? The timing related to the appearance of the flash drive couldn't be a coincidence. Had Abbie just stumbled on the item the Romola family was searching for?

"This could be what the Romolas are so desperate to get ahold of, couldn't it?" Abbie asked, echoing his thoughts.

Eyes narrowing, he nodded. "My gut tells me it could very well be. Vito would have had access to your case that night. We need to see what's on that flash drive."

"But why would he leave it with me when he planned to kill me? If he did leave it, then that would mean...what? And how did the Romolas even know the flash drive existed and that I had it in my possession when I didn't have a clue myself?"

Ethan rubbed his jaw thoughtfully. "I have no idea, but the contents of that drive should give us a better idea of what's going on here."

Excitement sparked in Abbie's eyes. "Let's head back to the chalet so we can plug it into my laptop."

Abbie hurriedly packed up her camera gear, and they rushed back to the house, where they filled Jaret in on her discovery. Abbie was grabbing her laptop to connect the flash drive when Zane trotted to the window, growling low in his throat.

Glancing up to see what had captured his dog's attention, Ethan spotted movement in the distance. Grabbing his binoculars, he sucked in a breath when the optic brought the threat into view. Three men with rifles were making their way through the woods toward the tree line bordering the house. "We've got company," he murmured urgently.

"Vince and his men?" Abbie asked, her voice cracking.

Ethan's didn't take his eyes off the rapidly approaching intruders. "Yeah, and they're packing some serious firepower."

"How did they find us so fast?" Abbie stammered.

"They couldn't have connected the dots to link this property to the Warden Service so quickly. The only way they could have tracked us here is if someone tipped them off," Ethan replied. "Only a handful of people knew we planned to use the chalet as a stopover on the way to the safe house."

"And they're all law enforcement officers," Jaret noted tersely. "The Romolas must have someone working for them inside the Warden Service or the NYPD."

"Or both," Ethan added gravely.

The pulse in Jaret's jaw ticked as his frustration percolated. "Which means we can't be sure the location of the NYPD safe house we're taking Abbie to hasn't been compromised. We're going to need a new plan."

Watching the men fan out along the edge of the woods, Ethan fisted his hands at his sides. "We'll have to come up with that plan on the fly. Once those men spread out and surround us, we'll be trapped. We've got to leave. Now."

"How are we going to make it to the helicopter without them spotting us?" Abbie asked.

Seeing her hands tremble as she hastily stowed her laptop and the flash drive in her bag, Ethan rushed to reassure her. "They're not going to see us." He pointed to the cellar door. "There's a trapdoor that opens to a tunnel. That tunnel leads to the helicopter pad."

"Time to move," Jaret warned. "They're closing in fast."

"Komm!" Ethan called to Zane. Leading the way downstairs to the finished basement, he strode over to the far wall. Bending down, he pulled back a corner of the rug to reveal a hidden door. Opening it, he used his flashlight to illuminate a staircase that led to a narrow, concrete passageway and then turned to Abbie. "Jaret is going to lead you out."

"What about you?" she stammered.

"As soon as I secure the trapdoor, Zane and I will be right behind you," Ethan assured her.

Turning on his flashlight, Jaret began to descend the staircase. He motioned to Abbie to join him, but she stood frozen in place.

Seeing her hesitancy, Ethan squeezed her shoulder gently in reassurance. "It's going to be okay."

"Be careful," she urged with a tremulous smile that made him even more determined to keep her safe no matter the cost.

"Always." He wanted to say more, but there wasn't time. He had to get her to safety before the men hunting her caught up with them.

EIGHT

Reaching the end of the secret corridor, Jaret cautiously opened the door. The cleverly camouflaged exit was situated a few hundred yards away from the helicopter pad. The storm front had moved out, the clouds rolling back to reveal the warm, golden glow of the late day sun. After surveying the perimeter and seeing no signs of a potential threat, he turned and flashed a thumbs-up. "All clear."

All too aware that their window of opportunity to make it to the chopper undetected could slam shut any second, Ethan turned to Abbie. "We're going to have to make a run for it. Jaret and I will go first to be sure no one is waiting to ambush us. Once we know it's safe, I'll signal you to join us."

Charging for the aircraft alongside Jaret, Ethan's concern that the men pursuing them would emerge from the cover of the forest to ambush them intensified with each stride. He prayed the men hadn't already come across the helicopter and sabotaged their ride out of here.

Reaching the helicopter unimpeded, Ethan locked eyes with Abbie and motioned her to head their way.

She broke into a sprint, but her healing leg wasn't up to the full-out pace she was attempting. Midway to the helicopter, the weak limb buckled, sending her tumbling to the ground.

Heart lurching, Ethan raced to her side to help her to her feet. "We've got to hurry," he urged, cradling her against him. "We're running out of time. Just lean on me."

Arriving at the helicopter, Ethan lifted her up into the passenger compartment and quickly fastened her seat belt before directing Zane to the spot beside her and securely buckling him in.

Rushing to the cockpit, he leaped into the pilot's seat and handed Abbie a headset. With a few deft flicks of the control switches, he brought the chopper whirring to life.

"I see movement through the trees," Abbie uttered on a worried breath. "I think they're coming."

"It's them," Jaret confirmed from his spot in the co-pilot's seat. "And they've spotted us!"

Jaw clenched in concentration, Ethan continued flipping switches in rapid succession. "Hang tight. We're getting out of here."

Murmuring a prayer for their safety, he took the helicopter skyward. Glancing at the ground below, his throat tightened. Their pursuers had their rifles at the ready and were taking aim at the chopper.

"They're going to shoot!" Abbie cried out.

Cringing as bullets whizzed past the helicopter's fuselage, Ethan directed the craft higher. Veering sharply away from the armed men below, he prayed the evasive maneuver would be enough to spare the helicopter from a hit that would certainly lead to a crash landing.

Abruptly banking the craft to avoid incoming fire, Ethan navigated the chopper safely past the barrage of bullets until their attackers faded to barely visible dots against the green landscape.

"You're still a show-off, I see," Jaret chuckled, rolling his eyes as he patted Ethan's shoulder.

"You're just jealous because my airmanship skills surpass yours," Ethan retorted, grinning broadly. Shifting in his seat, he turned his attention to Abbie and Zane. "Everything okay back there? How's the leg, Abbie?" he asked, concern lacing his voice.

"It feels better already," she assured him. "I just pushed too hard and the muscle seized." Pausing, she glanced at the German shepherd beside her. "Zane's doing great, too."

Ethan smiled his relief. "Good. It's time to regroup, then. We need a new plan."

"Yeah," Jaret agreed. "We can't use the NYPD's safe house now. There's no question we have a leak somewhere inside either my department or yours."

Ethan nodded in agreement. "I'm afraid so. The good news is I have an idea of what our next move might be. I have a friend who is a lighthouse keeper on an island here. I think it's the perfect spot for us to take refuge. I need to confirm it's doable first, so I'm going to set the chopper down when we reach that clearing up ahead. I'll call Hunter to make sure it's okay if we stay there for a few days."

Jaret raised an eyebrow skyward. "Island, huh? Please tell me we're headed someplace tropical."

"Afraid not. Although there is a beach—minus the palm trees and flamingos."

"That will do." Jaret grinned before his expression turned serious. "I think we'd better keep the location just between us. I'll let my department think I'm following the original plan. Since our mission has clearly been compromised, the fewer details we share, the better."

"Agreed," Ethan concurred.

Abbie sighed. "You know my thoughts on this. I'd prefer not to hide out at all. I don't want to waste time running from the Romola family. I want to go after them."

"I get it," Ethan sympathized. "I know the past few days have been a nightmare, and you're anxious to put an end to it. Trust me, Jaret and I want nothing more than to see the Romola family pay for their crimes, too. We're going to make that happen. First, we need to figure out what their endgame is so we can make a successful run at them. That starts with finding out what's on that flash drive."

After setting the helicopter down in the clearing, Ethan stepped out to make a phone call. He returned a few minutes later with good news. "I explained our predicament, and Hunter is on board and eager to help. Our plan B is a go."

"That's great," Jaret enthused as Ethan got them in the air again. "You're confident the island won't be on the Romola family's radar?"

"Not entirely," Ethan admitted ruefully. "They're resourceful, but it's as secure a spot as any at the moment. Hunter was in the military, so we'll have an extra set of trained eyes and ears on hand for backup should they discover our location."

"I hope it won't come to that," Abbie murmured. "Finding the flash drive is the first break we've gotten in this investigation. We need time to figure out what's on it."

Ethan nodded. "Given the lengths the Romolas are

willing to go to get ahold of it, the information it contains has to be incredibly damaging."

Jaret frowned. "Not to be a wet blanket, but you do realize that flash drive is almost certainly going to be password protected and the data on it encrypted? We're going to have to get past whatever security measures it's outfitted with before we can access the contents."

"Yeah," Ethan acknowledged. "And that's another good reason for us to travel to the island. Hunter is a cybersecurity expert."

Jaret's eyes widened. "Perfect. I can't wait to meet him."

Amusement lit Ethan's face. "Her," he corrected. "Hunter is a woman. And that's her house up ahead," he announced as a towering stone lighthouse perched adjacent to a Cape-style cottage with a white clapboard exterior came into view.

"It's gorgeous," Abbie enthused.

Ethan smiled. "You're going to love this place. The island is home to all sorts of wildlife. Hunter is also an artist, like you. A painter. Her specialty is landscapes, but she's also done some incredible portraits of the local flora and fauna."

"How did you two meet?" Abbie asked.

"Hunter served as a cryptographer in the Army. When she left active duty, she started her own business. I did a stint with the NYPD cybercrimes unit, and Hunter was called in as a consultant on a computer fraud incident. Thanks to her talent, we cracked the case."

"She sounds like a whiz," Jaret observed.

Ethan smiled. "That's an apt description. You'll get to

see for yourself in just a minute. I'm going to set us down on that dock up ahead."

He landed the helicopter on the narrow jetty. As soon as the rotors stopped whipping, he stepped out of the chopper and came around to help Abbie before collecting Zane.

Excited to have his paws on solid ground again, the dog tore off to explore.

"He won't get lost, will he?" Abbie frowned.

"He'll be fine," Ethan assured her with a chuckle. "He's been here before, and he knows he's not allowed to stray beyond the gated area. Hunter is probably in her studio working on a painting. Let's head around back."

As they rounded the rear of the structure, a petite blonde standing at an easel waved to them from the balcony at the top of the lighthouse. "Welcome. Come on up," she invited cheerfully.

Sea spray misted Abbie's face as she climbed the circular metal staircase to the main gallery of the lighthouse. Soaking in the panoramic view of the rocky coastline, she was transfixed by the raw beauty of the ocean. The sight and sound of the waves beating out a glorious symphony as they buffeted the craggy rocks surrounding the lighthouse was mesmerizing.

Hunter met them at the top of the stairs and wrapped Ethan in a warm hug. "It's so good to see you. And these must be the friends you told me about."

"I'd like you to meet NYPD detective Jaret Striker and my friend Abbie Renforth," Ethan introduced. "Sorry to impose on you like this. We appreciate you letting us stay with you on such short notice."

Excitement sparked in Hunter's warm brown eyes. "Impose? Are you kidding? I'm thrilled to have a little intrigue to break up the monotony. I miss the adrenaline rush of my military-ops days. And I can't wait to take a look at the flash drive you said you need help cracking. Why don't we eat first? I thought you might enjoy a traditional Maine lobster bake, so I've got lobster, corn, potatoes and kielbasa steaming over hot rocks under a bed of seaweed down at the beach."

"That sounds amazing." Abbie smiled. Pausing, she nodded at the easel, where Hunter's rendering of the après-storm seascape was so true to life that the waves she'd captured in shades of ocean green and Prussian blue seemed to surge off the canvas. "Before we go, may I take a closer look at the piece you're working on?"

Pleasure lit Hunter's face. "By all means. There's so much inspiration to be found on this island. I have more ideas for paintings than I have hours in a day."

Soaking in every nuance of Hunter's masterful artwork, Abbie could almost feel the wave splatter and hear the raucous cry of the seagulls. "It's simply stunning," she praised.

"Thank you. Ethan told me you're a photographer. I realize you have a lot going on right now, but if you have a bit of downtime tomorrow, I know a spot where you can get some great photos of the seals and puffins who call this island home."

"I'd love that."

"It's a plan, then." She beamed before turning to include Ethan and Jaret in the conversation. "Let's go down to the house. I'll show you your rooms, and then we can head to the beach for dinner."

When they reached the base of the lighthouse, Hunter gestured to the charming keeper's quarters. "Come on in. I'll give you a tour of the place. You can pick out your rooms for the night and freshen up."

Though the exterior of the home, with its whitewashed shingles, gabled roof and brick chimney, was quaint, the vibe inside the charming Cape was decidedly modern. Hardwood floors finished in the same dark gray stain as the heavy oaken beams that spanned the ceiling gleamed under beautiful pendant lights of sea green island art glass. In the living room, an expansive gray sectional positioned by a huge stone fireplace invited conversation. The ocean-hued toss pillows and cozy throws accessorizing the oversize sofa made it the perfect conversation and relaxation spot.

Once they'd chosen their rooms and settled in, Hunter took them down to the beach, where mouthwateringly delicious scents emanated from a seaweed-covered pit dug into the sand.

Soon, they were comfortably seated on a large blanket spread out on the beach.

"Ethan, would you say grace?" Hunter asked.

Nodding, Ethan bowed his head. "Heavenly Father, we thank You for seeing us safely through this day. Thank You for the blessing of these friends, and for this opportunity to gather with them amid the beauty of Your creation. We thank You for the food that You have provided that we are about to enjoy, and for the hands that prepared it. Amen."

"Amen," Jaret, Hunter and Abbie chorused.

Gazing longingly at the ear of corn in Ethan's hand, Zane begged enthusiastically for a sample.

"Okay, bud," Ethan surrendered, stripping some of the sweet, tender kernels from the ear of corn and putting them on a plate for the K-9. After scoffing the treat down, the German shepherd zipped back and forth exuberantly across the beach, pausing only to make friends with the seagulls and inspect pieces of driftwood washed up along the shore.

With the setting sun bedecking the sky in bright bands of crimson, magenta and gold, Ethan and Jaret built a campfire.

"Dessert, anyone?" Hunter asked, pulling bamboo skewers, chocolate bars and packages of graham crackers and marshmallows from her beach bag.

The tantalizing aromas of melting chocolate and warm graham crackers wrapped around them as they made s'mores over the fire.

When they'd finished, Hunter stood. "Is anyone up for a walk? The coastline at night is beautiful. I brought flashlights if anyone is interested in exploring."

Jaret rose to his feet. "I'm in."

Abbie surreptitiously massaged her calf. A walk sounded lovely, but her leg wasn't on the same page. The rigors of the past few days had left it tight and achy. "I'm too stuffed to move," she groaned. "I think I'll stay and enjoy the campfire."

"I'm in the too-stuffed-to-move camp, as well," Ethan replied. "I'll hang back here with Abbie. Enjoy the walk."

"We'll see you back at the house, then." Hunter smiled.

As Hunter and Jaret headed off down the beach, Ethan grabbed another marshmallow. Skewering it, he toasted it over the campfire until it turned a deep golden brown. Pulling the puffy, warm marshmallow off the stick, he sandwiched it between two graham crackers and a square of rich chocolate. Splitting the sweet treat in half, he handed her a piece.

"What happened to 'too stuffed to move'?" she teased.

"I may have found space for a few more s'mores. Can't let these marshmallows go to waste," he replied with a wink before growing serious. "I'm sorry your leg's bothering you. Is there anything I can do to help?"

His perceptiveness surprised her. "I'm fine. Just a little sore. Is that why you didn't go with the others? You didn't have to stay behind to keep me company."

"I know. I stayed because this is where I want to be."

His words warmed her even more than the heat radiating from the red-hot embers of the blazing campfire. Sitting next to Ethan by the crackling fire with a bright canopy of stars overhead, Abbie found herself focusing less on the terrifying events of the past couple of days and more on the man sharing this idyllic spot with her.

Realistically, she knew she was torturing herself with a sample of what could never be. But here, in this moment, it felt good to indulge in a happily-ever-after fantasy and forget about the evil men pursuing her. Even if the respite was only temporary.

"I'm glad you're here to help me figure this mess out. Reconnecting with you is the one bright spot in this unmitigated disaster."

Ethan's piercing blue eyes met hers. "I'm sorry for the circumstances that brought us together again. I wish you weren't being targeted by the Romola family, but I'm glad I'm here, too."

For a moment, Abbie let herself wonder whether the uncharacteristically husky note in his voice could be attributed to some depth of emotion he might feel toward her. She quickly snuffed out the ridiculous thought. It was just the wood smoke making him hoarse. Nothing more. But then she looked up and her gaze tangled with Ethan's over the flickering fire. The depth of feeling filling the captivating blue depths of his eyes stunned her.

Suddenly, hope sparked, blazing as brightly as the glowing embers in the campfire. A heartbeat later, Ethan's long, dark lashes shuttered his gaze, and his head dipped closer to hers. The movement brought their lips within brushing distance. He was close—so temptingly close. Was he going to kiss her?

"Woof! Woof!"

Barking gleefully and oblivious to his poor timing, Zane trotted up to them. Depositing a piece of driftwood at their feet, he sat watching them expectantly, his head cocked playfully.

Jolted by the interruption, Ethan drew away from her, looking as shell-shocked as she felt.

And, just like that, the spell was broken. Had Zane not interrupted them, would Ethan have closed the minuscule gap separating their lips? Would he have kissed her?

Determined not to let him see her disappointment at his abrupt withdrawal, Abbie forced a smile. "It looks like we're being recruited for a game of fetch."

Throwing the stick for Zane to chase, she chastised herself for letting her overactive imagination run wild. Of course the thought of kissing her hadn't crossed Ethan's mind. She'd completely misread the situation.

Tail wagging, Zane raced off in pursuit. Bounding back with his prize clamped firmly in his mouth, he deposited it triumphantly at her feet. She was about to throw it for him again when a faint pop sounded.

Sucker punched by dread, Abbie whipped toward Ethan. He was already on the move. Stepping in front of her to shield her, he drew his gun, his gaze sweeping the shoreline for the source of the threat.

"Is someone firing at us?" Abbie stammered.

"Not sure. Stay behind me," he ordered, his whispered command humming with urgency.

A heartbeat later, a second sharper pop rang out. A flare hissed skyward, bursting into a plume of red hued light. A distress signal, not someone firing at them.

Abbie's gaze darted to the ocean. The only vessel in sight was a sleek yacht, slowly cruising the coast. It didn't appear to be in trouble. Even at this distance she could hear the steady thrum of its engines. So who had fired the flare?

Before she could voice the question, Jaret and Hunter came sprinting across the beach, their expressions taut with concern.

"We saw a pontoon plane circling low along the shoreline," Hunter blurted breathlessly. "The pilot made several passes over the beach. Searching."

"We heard one of their engines cut out and saw them veer off toward the far side of the island to make an emergency landing," Jaret interjected. "They fired a couple of flares. The first was a dud, but the next one went off. They were signaling someone."

Ethan nodded toward the yacht. "Probably the occupants of that ship. It just blinked its lights. Like a coded message. They're working together."

Abbie's face drained of color. "It has to be the Romolas."

Ethan placed a steadying hand on her shoulder. "It's going to be okay. They don't know we're here."

Not yet, Abbie thought, her stomach twisting in a knot of unease. The flare's glow had dissipated, but the danger hadn't. Somewhere out there, the Romolas were regrouping and planning their next move.

Soon, they would resume their hunt.

NINE

Ethan woke at the crack of dawn. Rubbing his bleary eyes, he brushed away the stubborn cobwebs of fatigue. He'd tossed and turned for hours last night, his mind racing with a mix of unanswered questions and unfamiliar emotions.

After dinner, he, Jaret, Abbie and Hunter had worked well past midnight trying to break through the layers of security standing between them and the contents of the flash drive, but circumventing the device's multitiered protection measures had proven impossible.

One thing was clear: Vito, or whoever had left the flash drive in Abbie's camera bag, had been serious about safeguarding the data it contained. Whatever information the drive held, the data was sensitive enough to merit no-holds-barred encryption.

Exhausted by their unsuccessful efforts to gain access to the data, they'd agreed it would be best to get some rest and try again in the morning. But sleep had eluded him, held at bay by his burning need to unravel the conundrum Abbie was facing.

That need had warred with other burning needs as a mix of feelings entirely as complicated as those surrounding Abbie's baffling case had percolated to the surface despite his best efforts to squelch them.

He didn't want to acknowledge it, but he couldn't ignore the truth any longer. Though he'd tried to keep Abbie at arm's length, he'd come to think of her as a friend. If he was honest with himself, he wanted her to be an even deeper part of his life than that.

Somehow, she'd managed to break through the emotional fortress he'd erected around his heart. Despite his best intentions to the contrary, he'd allowed the line between duty and personal feelings to blur. He'd begun to form a bond with her—a bond he had to sever for her safety. Whether or not he wanted to.

Wearily swiping a hand across his face, Ethan prepared to face the day. The sooner he got ready, the quicker he could grab his morning cup of coffee. He needed the caffeine infusion to jostle his sleep-deprived brain and focus his thoughts back where they belonged—on the case he had to solve.

And when you crack that case, Abbie will go back to the new life she's building for herself. A life you can't be a part of.

Ignoring the too-close-to-home taunting of his subconscious, he quickly got ready. After breakfast, he'd take another shot at decrypting the flash drive with the others. With a bit of luck, they'd be successful this time. Hopefully whatever they discovered would help build an ironclad case against the Romola family.

Leaving his room, he met Jaret in the hallway.

"You look like you got as much sleep as I did," Ethan observed wryly, as they headed downstairs to join Abbie and Hunter.

Jaret nodded. "I've been trying to work out the logistics of how the flash drive ended up in Abbie's camera bag. Going with our theory that it could be the key to proving the Romola family's illegal dealings, whoever left it for Abbie to find has to be someone with inside knowledge of the sketchy side of the Romolas."

"Yeah. And there has to be some significance to them leaving it with Abbie, specifically. They could have just as easily passed it along anonymously to the police or the media. This is definitely personal. My money's on Vito being the culprit."

In the kitchen, they poured cups of coffee and grabbed seats at the table.

Ethan swallowed a sip of coffee and turned to Abbie. "I've been giving a lot of thought to what might have prompted someone to leave the flash drive with you instead of passing it along anonymously to law enforcement or a news agency. The last thing I want to do is have you revisit the nightmare you're trying to put behind you, but at this point every tidbit of information we can gather is critical. Did Vito say anything to you that might have indicated he was at odds with his family?"

Abbie considered the question for long moments before shaking her head. "No. He hardly spoke at all. The only thing I remember is how livid his eyes looked behind his mask. He was so very angry. It was like he'd kept his rage bottled up inside and he was finally letting it all erupt. He muttered something about how his perfect plan had been ruined. That's all he said. Why?"

Recalling the horror of the scene the night of the attack, Ethan swiped a hand across his eyes. "I think Vito might have abducted you because he wanted to pass incriminating information about his father on to you via that flash drive. He would have had an opportunity to put it in your camera case while you were unconscious, before I arrived on the scene."

"But he was going to kill me," Abbie murmured in bewilderment.

"What if he only wanted it to seem like he'd tried to eliminate you? What if he was acting under Edgar's orders, and he decided to defy him? I think Vito's plan was to make Edgar believe he'd tried to eliminate you, but failed. Vito wanted you to survive so you would find the flash drive. He knew you'd bring it to an expert who could decrypt it and then you'd act on its contents."

"That makes sense," Abbie nodded. "I never leave my photography gear unattended. My camera bag is always either at my home, in my vehicle or right by my side on a shoot. There's no way I would have missed someone breaking into my apartment or vehicle to get to it. That means whoever left that storage device would have placed it in my bag when I was too preoccupied to notice. There was only one time when I had it with me but I didn't have my eyes on it—the night Vito abducted me."

"I think Vito left it with you purposefully, too," Jaret chimed in. "We won't know for certain if the drive contains information proving the Romolas are a mob family until it's decrypted, but let's assume it does. There was no love lost between Edgar and Vito. Vito wanted to be accepted by his family, but Edgar treated him like an outsider. Vito may have gotten frustrated with perpetually trying to earn his father's favor and never succeeding."

Ethan nodded. "Until that night, Vito had carried out dozens of slayings. He could have killed Abbie when

I arrived on the scene, but he surrendered instead. He couldn't kill her because he needed her to live so she could act on the info on the drive once she found it."

Hunter frowned. "But why wouldn't Vito just go to the police himself if he wanted to expose his family?"

"I think he was afraid of Edgar and Vince," Jaret offered. "He knew they had contacts everywhere. He couldn't go to the media or the authorities and remain anonymous."

"The pieces fit," Abbie murmured. "With the mask hiding Vito's identity, I wouldn't have been able to identify him. All he had to do was abduct me, plant the flash drive in my camera case and then make his escape. Once he was away from the scene, he could place a call to get help to me."

Deep in thought, Ethan rubbed a hand across his jaw. "Unfortunately, the theory still leaves us with a boatload of unanswered questions. How did the shooter know where Vito would be that night? Why did they want him dead? And who was that person who pulled the trigger and ended his life?"

Abbie's eyes widened. "I just remembered something. While Vito was tying me up, he was mumbling something. I think he said, 'I shouldn't have trusted her.'"

"Identifying the *her* Vito was talking about could shed more light on things," Ethan ventured.

Jaret nodded. "We should go back over the files from that night to see if there's anything the investigators might have overlooked."

"And I'll take another shot at getting into that flash drive," Hunter added.

Hours later, Hunter heaved a defeated sigh. "I'm really sorry. I'm not a quitter, but I'm willing to admit when I've been bested. I've tried every trick in my arsenal, but I can't crack the encryption. With your permission, I'd like to dial in one of my former counterparts. If anyone can get us access, he can."

"Absolutely," Ethan agreed.

After making the call, Hunter returned with news. "Brock is neck-deep in a time-sensitive project at the moment, so he can't come to us. He says if I can bring the drive to him, he's happy to take a look at it. He's a two-hour drive away, in Portland."

"That works," Jaret replied. "I'll go with you. We can take the helicopter. It'll save us time on the road. We can rent a car when we get there. Given how rabid the Romola family is to get their hands on the flash drive, I'll feel better if you aren't traveling solo."

"Me, too," Ethan agreed. "I'll stay here with Abbie. Portland is a heavily populated area. We can't take the risk that someone with connections to the Romola family might spot her."

"But I want to help," Abbie protested.

"You are helping," Ethan replied. "We need to make sure you stay off the Romola family's radar."

"I could take you to see the seals, if you'd like, while Ethan and Jaret finish reviewing the case notes. We have time before Jaret and I have to leave to meet Brock."

Abbie's face brightened at the suggestion. "That would be amazing! I'd love the chance to photograph them."

"Hunter, I take it you're proficient with the rifle I saw in your gun cabinet?" Jaret asked.

"Proficient enough to earn the Army's distinguished shooter badge," she replied with a cheeky grin.

"Great! Zane can tag along with you and Abbie as an extra measure of protection," Ethan replied. "He can't resist chasing foxes, but he won't bother the seals or the seabirds."

"If you ride, we could take my horses," Hunter suggested.

"I do, but it's been a while."

"My boys are true gentlemen." Hunter grinned. "You can ride Tucker. He's incredibly easygoing, and he knows all the trails on the island by heart."

"Great!" Abbie enthused. "I'll go grab my camera."

When Abbie returned with her gear, Ethan called Zane to his side and directed the K-9 to guard her and Hunter. Watching his partner head out the door with the women, he was secure in the knowledge that between Zane's protection skills and Hunter's military training, Abbie was secure.

He was glad she was getting a chance to put the insanity of the past few days aside for a while. He'd like nothing more than to go along on their seal-watching adventure, if only to see her enjoyment of the island's wildlife. But he couldn't. There was work to be done.

When Abbie and Hunter entered the barn, the resident horses greeted them with welcoming nickers. The smell of fresh hay sweetened the air inside the pristine stable. Two striking geldings poked their heads out of adjacent stalls in friendly curiosity, their intelligent eyes perfectly framed by long, dark lashes. The smaller of the two horses tossed his ebony head in their direction, the movement sending his long, silky mane dancing.

"What a beauty," Abbie smiled.

"That's Tucker. And the handsome-and-he-knows-it pinto in the stall next to him is Clancy. I'll saddle him, and then I'll help you saddle Tucker."

Between the horsemanship tips Hunter shared and Tucker's infinitely patient demeanor, they were soon on their way. In stark contrast to the stormy weather of the day before, the sun was warm and bright. A soft breeze carried the fresh tang of salt and seaweed, and Zane followed along happily beside them.

"Oh!" Abbie exclaimed softly as she caught her first glimpse of the harbor seal colony sunbathing on the rocks at the ocean's edge. When she and Hunter dismounted and settled down on a large, flat boulder a nonthreatening distance away, dozens of pairs of liquid ebony eyes tracked their movements curiously.

Dropping down on the rock for a better angle, Abbie captured image after image of the adorable, long-whiskered baby seals and their proud parents amid the background music of their barks and honks.

"Best photo shoot ever," Abbie pronounced after capturing dozens of images of the delightful creatures. "Talk about cuteness overload."

Hunter beamed. "If you think this is the epitome of cuteness, wait until you see the puffins. Their chicks are called pufflings, and they're just as adorable as their name implies. Prepare to have your heart stolen."

After capturing an entire SD card's worth of photos, Abbie turned to Hunter. "Thanks for sharing this with me. You're so lucky to call this place home."

"I'm grateful I get to live here. Landing the lighthouse caretaker job has been a blessing. Speaking of blessings,

I hope Ethan realizes how fortunate he is to have you in his life."

Abbie shook her head. "Oh, we're not a couple. I'm not even sure Ethan thinks of me as a friend."

Hunter guffawed. "Right. I don't buy that. I've known Ethan for a long time, and I've never seen him look at a woman the way he looks at you."

Cheeks flaming, Abbie dipped her head. This was the second stranger who'd assumed she and Ethan were in a relationship.

"He doesn't think of me that way. Trust me."

"The man clearly has feelings for you. He might not want to admit he does, but his body language tells a completely different story. And you care about him, too, don't you?"

Recalling how quickly Ethan had exited her life after her release from the hospital, Abbie's face crumpled. "Even if I did, it wouldn't matter. I'm just an assignment to him. I made the mistake of thinking he might want to be a part of my life once before. I won't make that mistake again." Entirely trusting of this caring, thoughtful woman she already thought of as a friend, Abbie found it was easy to open up to her about her past. "I know that sounds harsh, but I've had the rug pulled out from under me too many times when it comes to relationships. Growing up, I never knew my father. He was a random guy my mother got involved with, and they were both addicted to drugs. He died before I was born.

"My mother stayed clean for a while, but she eventually fell back into her former habits. The pull of her addiction was so strong that nothing else mattered to her.

After she lost her life to that addiction, I was placed in a foster home. The first of many."

"I'm sorry," Hunter murmured.

"I'm not telling you this so you'll feel sorry for me. I just want you to understand why I can't let myself get attached to Ethan. When he first came into my life, I thought I'd found someone who would stay. I was wrong. The only reason he's even here with me right now is because he has a job to do."

"But he hasn't run away this time, has he?"

Abbie stood to stretch her tight leg muscles. "That's only because he can't. He's been assigned to protect me, and Ethan never runs from his responsibilities. When he wraps up this assignment, he'll move on. And that's for the best, really." Pausing, she bent down and pushed up the left leg of her jeans. Running her fingers over the puckered scars she swallowed back the painful memories that reared their ugly head every time she saw the jagged ridges that zigzagged across her skin. "He deserves better than me," she said, her voice cracking. "The attack left physical scars, and I bear the emotional scars to match. I'm working to get past that, but I don't know how long it will take before I reach a point where I can truly put what happened that night behind me. God knows I'm trying to. Anyhow, considering the mess I am, if I were Ethan I'd run from me, too."

Seeing the deep etchings marring Abbie's leg, Hunter's lips pursed in a grim line. "I'm so sorry for what that monster did to you, but those scars don't make you any less attractive. They're a badge of courage. I can guarantee you that's how Ethan sees them. He doesn't care about your outward appearance—which is beautiful, by the way."

Pausing, she covered her heart with her hand. "It's what's in here that matters to him. And you are gorgeous both inside and out."

With a grateful smile, Abbie pushed the denim back down to cover her leg. "Thanks."

"Ethan has scars of his own, you know. They're not physical ones, but they're just as raw. I'm not sure if you know this, but he was engaged once. It ended badly. His fiancée never showed up for their wedding. She was in love with someone else, and she was carrying on the relationship behind Ethan's back. The entire time she and Ethan were planning their wedding, she was leading a double life. At the last possible moment, she decided to come clean. She left him standing at the altar."

"I had no idea. How awful for him. He must have been crushed when he learned the truth."

"Crushed is an understatement. He kind of went off the rails for a while. It took some time before he found his way back."

"So, he still has feelings for her?"

Hunter shook her head adamantly. "Oh, no. He realizes what happened was for the best. Sondra is happily married now, and Ethan has long since forgiven her. I just wanted you to have some context for why he's so guarded when it comes to opening his heart to anyone."

"I can see how that kind of a betrayal would make him reluctant to let someone close. She violated his trust. No wonder he's walled off his heart."

Hunter hummed in agreement. "He also has a habit of assuming responsibility for things outside of his control. He's carrying a lot of weight on his shoulders that isn't his to bear. He blames himself for what happened to his partner, Gabriella. And he's convinced he could have prevented the Spitting Image Slayer from striking again the night you were attacked if he'd arrived sooner."

"What happened to Gabriella was tragic, but there's no way Ethan could have saved her. And, ultimately, he ended the Slayer's killing spree."

"You and I know that. Ethan doesn't see it that way. He blames himself for those scars you bear. In his mind, he's a failure. He holds himself responsible for Gabriella's death and for the death of the woman Vito attacked along with you."

Abbie's eyes widened. "There's no way he could have saved Leanne. She was already gone when Vito brought her to the site where he planned to bury us. I think she reacted badly to whatever drug he injected her with to sedate her."

An urgent bark from Zane interrupted their conversation. Eyes darting to the K-9, they saw him looking up at the sky.

Hunter scanned the azure expanse stretching out above them for any indication something was amiss. "I don't see anything, do you?" she asked.

"No," Abbie replied as Zane continued to bark insistently. "What is it, boy?"

Hunter tilted her head, listening intently. "Do you hear that?"

"Hear what?" No sooner had she responded, Abbie registered a low-pitched hum, barely audible over the noisy concerto of Zane's booming alarm and the waves thundering against the rocky cliffside. "Oh! Now I hear it. It sounds like a drone. I don't see anything, though."

Scanning the sky, Hunter pointed to a black speck in

the distance. "There it is! It *is* a drone! I'm sure it doesn't belong to anyone on this island. Only a handful of people live here, and none of them are tech aficionados. They don't have any need for a drone."

Abbie inhaled sharply. "This has the Romolas written all over it. They're using the drone to search for me!"

TEN

Eyes glued to the craft circling overhead, Abbie's heart thudded in her chest as the buzz of fast-whirling rotors drew closer. Each sweep the drone made across the sky increased the odds that she and Hunter would be discovered.

An involuntary shudder snaked down her spine. "We need to hide."

Hunter pointed to a dense pine grove that bordered the rocky ledge. "Let's take Zane and the horses to the tree line so we're not out in the open. Then, we'll see if my sharpshooting skills are still on point."

Reaching the cover of the woods, Hunter drew her rifle from the scabbard mounted to her horse's saddle. Snapping the safety off, she aimed at the hovering craft and squeezed the trigger.

With a loud crack, a bullet soared to its mark. Exploding under hit, the disabled craft plummeted from the sky.

"Threat eliminated," Hunter pronounced with satisfaction as Zane raced to check out the downed wreckage. "We'd better get back to the house before whoever was piloting the drone comes looking for it. Do you know what the range of a craft like that is?"

Abbie considered the drone's remains. "It looks like it

was a fairly high-tech model. My guess is the pilot could be as far as eight miles away. Of course, they could be closer…"

"Ethan and Jaret will have heard the rifle blast. They'll be worried. Let's go fill them in."

The men had indeed registered the disturbance. Driving utility task vehicles, they met Abbie and Hunter on the trail.

Waving to them, Abbie and Hunter reined in their horses and dismounted as Ethan and Jaret cut their engines.

"We heard a shot. Are you guys okay?" Ethan blurted, concern clouding his face.

"We're fine," Abbie assured him. "Zane alerted us to a drone that was surveilling the area. We figured the Romolas were using it to search for us, so Hunter shot it down. She was brilliant."

"Great work," Jaret praised.

Ethan nodded. "Yes. Your quick thinking bought us some time."

"Edgar and Vince aren't going to give up until they get their hands on that flash drive," Jaret wryly stated the obvious. "We're going to have to come up with a plan C."

Frustrated, Ethan plowed a hand through his hair. "Getting that flash drive to Hunter's friend is our top priority. We can't veer from that part of the plan. But Abbie and I are going to need to relocate. Stat."

Hunter tilted her head as she considered the options. "There's a national park a couple of hours drive away. You can take my van. I keep it stocked for impromptu camping trips, so it's already packed with everything you'll need. The Romolas won't connect my vehicle to you, so they won't be able to track you."

"That will work," Ethan affirmed. "Thank you. We should get back to the house. The sooner we head out, the better."

Abbie was about to mount her horse when she heard Zane growl. Turning, she saw him staring intently at the trail behind them, his hackles raised. The thrumming of a powerful engine sounded in the distance. A vehicle was approaching. Fast.

"That sounds like an off-road motorcycle," Ethan murmured, turning to Hunter. "Are these trails frequently used by the island residents?"

"No. All the trails on the lighthouse property are private."

Abbie's stomach clenched. The motorcyclist had to be connected to the Romolas. They'd seen enough via the drone before Hunter shot it down to pinpoint her location, and they'd found her! Now she and her friends were in a tight spot. The horses couldn't outrun a dirt bike, and the UTVs were slower and less agile than the motorcycle.

Ethan pointed to the UTVs. "Ladies, you'll ride back with us."

"What about the horses?" Abbie asked.

Hunter waved a hand, unconcerned. "Tucker and Clancy know these trails by heart. We'll bundle the reins around their saddles and they'll make their way back to the stable on their own. They'll be fine."

"Barn," she commanded the horses once their reins were dealt with, sending them back to their stable. Obeying the directive without hesitation, the two geldings galloped off toward home.

Hunter was nearest to Jaret. She jumped in the passenger seat of his UTV while Abbie boarded Ethan's machine. Ethan rushed to open the dog crate strapped to the back of his UTV and signaled Zane to climb in before hastily firing up the machine and leading the way down the trail.

The wail of a revving motor, fast approaching, made it clear their pursuer was gaining on them rapidly. "He's getting closer!" Abbie exclaimed.

"Don't worry," Ethan assured her. "What these UTVs lack in speed and agility, they make up for in stability. That motorcyclist won't be familiar with these trails. That gives us the upper hand. Just hang on."

With a twist of the throttle, Ethan sent the powerful machine surging forward. After checking to make sure Jaret was keeping up, he veered off onto a narrower trail that snaked along the cliffside.

For a few minutes, it seemed as though they'd lost the motorcyclist, but then the scream of an engine shrieked out behind them.

"Oh, no," Abbie breathed. "He's back."

No sooner had she uttered the warning, a shot rang out.

"Stay low," Ethan cautioned, weaving back and forth to deter the shooter. "There's a turnoff to another trail up ahead. It leads to a hill, and there's a deep rut on the other side where water collects. There's always a nasty mud pit in that area. It's a treacherous spot. We'll use that to our advantage."

Ethan's calm assuredness sent a wave of hope washing over Abbie. Though the motorcyclist continued to fire at them, Ethan's skillful maneuvering prevented their pursuer from getting a bead on them.

Abbie was amazed at how unruffled Ethan remained

in the face of danger. It was all she could do to hold back the tidal wave of pitiable thoughts threatening to drown her, but Ethan somehow always managed to stay calm in the midst of the tempest. Without uttering a word, his steady spirit reminded her that rather than struggling to keep her head above a torrent of *why me*s and *why now*s, she should be counting her blessings. God was here with her through this trial. And she firmly believed He'd sent a man she trusted and believed in to help see her through this storm. *Ethan.*

Shifting to maintain her balance as the UTV's tires clawed for traction, sending mud spraying in all directions, she clung to the side of the vehicle as Ethan skillfully navigated the steep ascent. Reaching the top of the gnarly hill, he opened the throttle. Speeding down the other side, he directed the UTV across the treacherous water crossing, positioning the wheels so the big machine was straddling the narrow strips of ground on either side of the slippery pit. Turning in her seat, she saw Jaret following behind them.

Once they were safely across the muddy ravine, Ethan and Jaret swung their UTVs onto another branch of the trail that skirted the cliffside and the ocean below. Spinning their machines around, they parked to face the approaching motorcyclist.

Abbie watched, her heartbeat thundering in her ears, as the helmeted rider raced toward them. The instant the motorcycle's front tire hit the swampy gully, it dropped into the cement-like goop and was swallowed up by the muck. The unexpected and abrupt stop sent the driver catapulting over the handlebars and into the miry pit.

Drawing their weapons, Ethan and Jaret aimed them

at the man who'd now abandoned his disabled machine and was slogging his way out of the muddy hole.

"Toss down your gun and don't take another step," Ethan ground out.

Rather than complying with the order, the man lunged for dry ground, extricating himself from the muck in one bound. The moment his boot landed on solid footing, he bolted for the cliff, launching himself off the rocky ledge into the deep, roiling water below.

Horrified, Abbie looked down at the turbulent water. The motorcyclist surfaced once. Twice. And then he was gone.

"No!" she cried out, trembling in reaction to the tragedy she'd just watched unfold.

"There wasn't anything we could have done to save him, Abbie," Ethan murmured in consolation, drawing her close to his side. "He picked his path."

Her gaze fixed on the churning waves that had swallowed the man, Abbie let herself lean into the comforting support of Ethan's arms as her knees threatened to buckle. "I can't believe he chose to die rather than fail at his mission. How can the Romolas wield that much power over the people they hire to do their dirty work?"

Ethan shook his head, his jaw tightening in resolve. "The Romolas manipulate loyalty and use it as a weapon. But I promise I won't let them hurt you."

Abbie clenched her hands, willing them to stop shaking. "Whatever it is they want from me, surely it isn't worth the cost. I didn't ask for this. I don't want to be the reason lives are lost."

Seeing Abbie's hands tremble, Ethan's gut clenched. He wished he could have shielded her from the icy horror of what she'd just witnessed. Regret left him feeling hollow. Yet another life had been lost to the Romola family's wicked rampage.

Logically, he understood the motorcyclist could have chosen to turn himself in rather than take his own life. Still, he wished he'd foreseen the man's intent. Maybe he could have talked him out of it.

Shaking himself from his musings, he turned to the others. "We'd better head back. There's a good chance he isn't alone. I'll call the authorities and report the incident when we get back to the house."

Upon arriving at the lighthouse, Ethan let Zane out of his dog crate, commanding the K-9 to guard the perimeter of the property. Though it appeared the man had acted alone, Ethan wasn't willing to chance it. Keeping Abbie safe was his top priority.

Confident his K-9 partner would alert at the slightest indication of potential trouble, he went inside with the others and called the State Police to report the attack and their assailant's subsequent fatal dive off the cliffside.

After dispensing with the necessary reporting requirements in the aftermath of the incident, Ethan went to find Abbie. She'd gone to her room to pack.

Poking his head into her room, he knocked softly on the door frame to get her attention. "Can I lend a hand with anything?"

Looking up from zipping her travel bag, she sent him a grateful smile. "Thanks, but I'm all set. I'm ready to go whenever you are."

That smile. It did things to him. It made him feel things he had no business feeling—not when it came to Abbie. She cared about him. He wasn't blind to that. But it was for that exact reason he had to keep their relationship strictly on friends-only footing. It was that or risk breaking the heart she'd opened so freely to him. Or having his own heart broken.

After the debacle with Sondra, he'd vowed to never let anyone get close to him again. But Abbie was different. She'd broken through his defenses, blasting through his armor and blurring the lines between friendship and something more despite his valiant efforts to keep her at arm's length.

He hadn't meant to get attached to her, but he realized now just how important she'd become to him. That scared him more than anything.

Having her in his life in any capacity was a blessing he wasn't worthy of. He didn't deserve that kind of a gift—especially not when it was offered by a woman as special as Abbie. He'd done nothing to merit her unquestioning faith in his goodness. He wasn't worthy of her love. He wasn't the man she thought he was.

The agony she'd endured, and the pain she still lived with because he'd failed her, was something he could never forgive himself for. If he hadn't been so focused on exacting revenge for his partner's senseless murder, he quite possibly could have spared her the tremendous suffering she'd endured at the Spitting Image Slayer's hands.

"Ethan? Is everything all right?" Abbie questioned softly, drawing him from his musings.

"Everything's fine." He stepped forward and held his hand out to take her travel bag. "Here. Let me carry that for you."

"Thanks. And not just for offering to carry my bag.

Thank you for everything you've done and that you are doing for me. I'm sorry you got dragged into this mess."

Ethan reached out to take the bag she handed him, and their fingers brushed. He quickly pulled away. Hearing her soft intake of breath, he knew the abruptness of his withdrawal hadn't gone unnoticed. His reaction had stung her, and he hated that it had. But even the most innocent contact with her had a way of muddling his thoughts. Now, more than ever, he couldn't afford to have his focus splintered.

Abbie's lips quivered. "When this is over, you're going to leave again, aren't you? You'll just drop out of my life again, like you did before."

The certainty with which she uttered the statement was like a kick to his gut. He swallowed, his heart lurching at the pain swimming in her beautiful green eyes as they locked questioningly on his. "I can't stay."

Tipping her chin up, she blinked back tears. "Why not?"

He hesitated, grasping for a way to make her understand that people close to him always got hurt. Friends, family, even colleagues—no one was safe around him. Even now that he'd chosen to serve in a less hazardous branch of law enforcement, there was still always the chance that an enemy from his past could surface in search of revenge. He couldn't bear it if anyone he loved got hurt as a result of that.

"The work I do is kryptonite when it comes to relationships. I know you don't understand why I felt I had to drop out of your life, but it was the right decision. When my mission here is complete, it will be the right decision then, too."

Seeing her brush away a tear, Ethan's chest constricted. Her heart was mirrored in her beautiful green gaze. All the broken bits. It gutted him to think that he was the one responsible for causing that devastation. He glanced down at the floor, the hurt on her face too much to bear. "You make me feel things I haven't felt in a very long time. Things I can't allow myself to feel. If I stay, I'm afraid I might not be able to walk away again. And I *have* to walk away. I'm sorry."

Resigned, she simply nodded. "Well, I'm glad you're here, for now. After seeing the lengths the Romola family is willing to go to in order to make sure I'm out of the picture, I'm so very thankful you're here to help me fight back against them. And I'm thankful for your friends who've rallied around to help. I never wanted to involve anyone else, but I'm grateful I'm not alone in this battle."

"You're never alone," Ethan asserted. "God's got this."

"I know. He sent you to save me once. I believe He's sent you again."

Ethan's pulse stuttered when Abbie lightly placed her hand on his arm to punctuate her heartfelt words. The warm brush of her fingers sent a lightning bolt of emotion zipping through him. He wanted nothing more than to dip his head to close the scant distance between their lips and kiss her. But he couldn't. Wouldn't.

Reminding himself why he couldn't do this, he reluctantly drew away. He wasn't worthy of her faith in him. He didn't deserve her trust. Stepping back to put more distance between them, he moved to the door. He didn't miss the disappointment that flitted across her face at his hasty withdrawal.

"I'm sorry," he apologized again, feeling like a heel.

"That was my fault. I didn't mean to send you mixed signals."

Face crumpling, she shrugged, trying to feign indifference but failing miserably. "No. I'm the one who should be apologizing. You just told me you don't want to get involved with me. I have a habit of forgetting everything when I'm around you. I won't make that mistake again."

Now he'd hurt her feelings, which was the last thing he'd wanted to do. It was a tricky path he was treading, trying to remain indifferent to the things she made him feel. "I'm not the right guy for you, Abbs."

Hot color flamed in her cheeks. "Don't worry. I get it. I'm scarred. I don't blame you for not being interested in me."

Not interested in her? Was that what she thought? Remembering the moment he'd first laid eyes on her, he realized he'd been drawn to her, even then, in the midst of that horrific situation. The more he'd gotten to know her, the more that initial fascination had taken on deeper layers of respect and admiration.

"I'm not repulsed by your scars. When I look at you, all I see is a gorgeous, brave, strong, compassionate woman. A woman who deserves better than a guy like me. Nothing Vito Romola did to you could dull your beauty."

"Then why did you bail?" she pressed, stammering. "You dropped out of my life without even a single word of explanation."

Ethan sucked in a wounded breath. "I never meant to hurt you. But I couldn't be a part of your life. I'd failed you. Those scars you bear are on me."

"How can you even think that? You didn't carve those marks into my skin. Vito did."

Regret blazed hot in Ethan's brilliant blue eyes. "I'm the reason they're there. When I received the anonymous tip that night, I should have acted quicker. I wasted time verifying it, trying to dot i's and cross t's and come up with a foolproof plan to get the Slayer on my own. If I hadn't gotten wrapped up in confirming every little detail, I would have arrived on the scene sooner. I might have been able to save Leanne and stop Vito before he could hurt you."

"It's a miracle you found us at all. And there was no way you could have saved Leanne. She was gone long before Vito brought us to the spot where he planned to bury us. She'd taunted him the entire time he was driving us to the spot. She kept pushing his buttons until he snapped. He was furious. He yanked the car to the side of the road and got a syringe from the glove box. He stabbed the needle in her arm and injected her with something. Whatever drug that syringe contained, she reacted badly to it. Or maybe he gave her too much. I'm not sure which. She died instantly.

"When Vito realized Leanne was dead, he fell into a rage. He made me dig two graves while he watched."

Ethan's stomach twisted at the remembrance of what she'd endured. Needing to redirect his focus, he checked his watch. "We'd better get going. Hunter and Jaret will be waiting."

Making their way downstairs, they joined up with Hunter and Jaret and left the house. While the other two headed to the helicopter, he and Abbie loaded their bags in the back of the Hunter's van so they'd be ready to leave to catch the ferry as soon as they returned from the short walk to the chopper.

"Komm!" he called to his partner. Zane bounded to him and sat at his feet, his head cocked alertly. "Good boy," he praised. Starting the van, he turned the air-conditioning on before seeing him settled in the vehicle. Then he and Abbie headed for the helicopter pad to see Jaret and Hunter off.

"Be careful, buddy," Jaret called from the pilot's seat. "I'll be in touch as soon as Hunter's friend gets us access to whatever's on the flash drive."

"Sounds good. Watch your back out there."

After waving goodbye, Jaret brought the craft roaring to life. Ethan and Abbie covered their ears with their hands against the roar of the rapidly spinning blades as they watched the helicopter lift off. Soaring higher and higher, it quickly disappeared from sight.

Hearing Abbie whisper a prayer for Hunter and Jaret's safety, Ethan joined in. Folding his fingers around her hand, he squeezed it gently in reassurance. "They're going to be okay. No one knows they have the flash drive except us. And Jaret won't let anything happen to either Hunter or that drive."

"I know," she replied, her eyes bright with unshed tears. "I just wish this was over."

"Me, too. It will be soon. I promise. I'm positive that flash drive holds the evidence we need to build a solid case against Edgar and Vince."

No sooner than he'd uttered the words, a loud crack rang out. Abbie spun around to face him, her gaze frantically telegraphing a question she didn't need to give voice to. Had the Romolas found them?

A pulse beat later, a plume of orange hued smoke billowed skyward. "A flare," he pronounced, rushing to alleviate her fears. "Probably a hiker or hikers in need of help. The trails around the lighthouse are private, but that doesn't always deter the locals." He hesitated, torn between his game warden duties and his assignment to protect Abbie. It would only take a moment for him to check out the situation, but he didn't want to leave her alone.

As if sensing his internal battle, Abbie waved a hand toward the woods. "Go. I'll hang back since I can't move as fast as you. The signal was close. It won't take you long to check on them. I'll be fine here," she insisted.

His gaze flicked to his watch again. Abbie was right. The flare had gone off mere yards away. He could check the situation out and still make it back in time to catch the ferry. He hesitated a moment longer, waging an inner battle between his desire to protect Abbie and his duty not to ignore anyone in need of help. Reluctantly, he bent to the urge to make sure the signalers were safe. "Okay, but don't wander off. I'll be right back."

Nodding her agreement, she smiled and sent him a thumbs-up.

Oh, the things that smile did to him. His heart lurched as another chunk of steel toppled from the barricade he'd erected around it. Shoving that distracting realization to the furthest recesses of his mind, he headed into the woods. Following the trail of colored smoke still billowing into the air, he soon found himself in a clearing. A spent casing told him he'd found the spot where the flare was issued. There wasn't a soul in sight. The only indication that anyone had been here was the empty casing, the boot-scuffed ground and a few snapped branches. The footprints indicated at least two men had stood in this spot. Maybe three. Unease skittered down his spine.

Had the distress call been a ruse, intended to separate him from Abbie?

As the sickening thought gained traction, so did his conviction he'd been set up, lured away so Abbie would be vulnerable. This was the Romola family's handiwork. And she was the only person who needed to be rescued.

Veering in the direction he'd come from, he bolted for lighthouse. With every frantic beat of his heart, fear for Abbie thrummed through him. He never should have left her!

He'd nearly reached the edge of the woods when he heard her terrified scream. His first instinct was to charge out of the tree line, but based on the prints he'd seen, he was surely outnumbered. He'd have the best chance of rescuing Abbie if he knew what he was dealing with first.

Surreptitiously making his way to the edge of the clearing, he peered through the thick underbrush. Abbie was flanked by Vince Romola and one of his goons. They were holding her at gunpoint.

Doing his best to tamp down the rage roaring through his blood at the sight of her trapped and at their mercy, Ethan considered his next move. They hadn't spotted him yet. He had the element of surprise on his side. But he was outgunned. If he only had himself to worry about, he wouldn't hesitate to take action. But with Abbie in the mix, he couldn't risk acting recklessly. She was in far too vulnerable a spot.

With Zane in the van, his options were limited. He could circle around behind the men and fire a shot in an attempt to incapacitate Vince or his henchman, but he couldn't risk her getting caught in the firefight that would inevitably break out.

The only other move he could think of was to set up a decoy to fake them out and draw their attention away from Abbie. Quietly moving back into the woods, he located a downed tree branch. Shedding the windbreaker he wore over his uniform shirt, he draped it around the tall, forked piece of wood so it resembled a human torso.

Stealthily slipping closer to Vince and his associate, he set the decoy up against a large fir tree. Stepping back several yards from his impromptu prop, he fired a shot in the air to draw the men's attention and then soundlessly circled around to the opposite side of them.

At the report of the gun blast, the men spun around. Mistaking the decoy for him as he'd counted on them doing, they opened fire on the dummy.

With the men's attention focused on eliminating the perceived threat, he could take action without putting Abbie in more danger. As he began to step out to confront them, he heard a twig snap behind him. A second later, he felt the cold press of steel against his back.

"Gotcha," his assailant snapped in his ear. "You're not the only one who knows how to be stealthy. Drop your weapon. Slowly, now, and no funny business or I'll reconsider my inclination to let you live. Mr. Romola gave us strict instructions that we're to take you and your lady friend alive. That doesn't mean you can't have an unfortunate accident."

With no choice but to comply, Ethan followed the man's orders.

Snickering, his assailant jabbed the gun into his back to prod him forward. "Let's go see my boss, shall we?"

"Ethan!" Abbie cried out when she spotted him emerging from the woods in front of the gunman. "Are you all right?"

"I'm fine," Ethan assured her as the assailant who had managed to sneak up on him gave him a shove, directing him to stand next to her.

Vince strolled over to them, his hard, cold gaze bouncing between them. "You two should have left well enough alone," he growled.

Squaring her shoulders, Abbie met his gaze. "You don't scare me."

He snorted in disbelief. "No? Well, you should be scared. If you haven't noticed, I'm the one holding all the cards. You have something of mine. I want it back."

"I don't know what you're talking about," Abbie replied.

"She doesn't have anything that belongs to you," Ethan ground out.

"Oh, but she does. Your lovely Abbie knows what I want. The sooner she turns it over to me, the better this will go for both of you."

Undaunted, Abbie held her ground. "Like I told you, I don't have any idea what you're talking about."

Vince hovered over her, malice turning his eyes to ice. "Did you really think you can mess with my family's business without there being any fallout? I know you have the flash drive. There's no point in denying it. I'm out of patience, so I'm going to ask one last time. Where is it?"

Ethan balled his fingers into fists, staring Vince down. "Abbie doesn't have what you're looking for. There's obviously been a mistake."

Vince scowled, unimpressed. "My brother, Vito, left behind a journal that says otherwise. Turns out he was quite the diarist. Did you know he liked to capture every detail of his killings in writing? Quite the unhinged ramblings, actually. His last journal entry was different. More lucid. It detailed his plan to make our father pay for treating him like an outcast."

"I don't see why that would make you think I have your storage device," Abbie retorted.

"Ah. But you see, you were the key to my brother's scheme to undermine our father. Edgar tasked him with eliminating you. Vito hoped by carrying out his orders he'd finally earn our father's respect. When Vito realized no matter what he did, he'd never gain his acceptance, he devised a plan to get back at him—with you at the center of it."

Abbie shook her head. "That makes no sense. Vito tried to kill me, remember?"

Vince shrugged. "He may have gotten a bit carried away, but he was never going to let you die. He needed you alive. He left a flash drive in your camera case. He needed you to keep breathing so you'd find it. He knew when you did, you'd find a specialist to crack its encryption and use the information on it to expose our father's illegal dealings."

"If he wanted to get even with Edgar, surely there was an easier way," Abbie asserted. "He could have just mailed the drive to me or the authorities. But if you're convinced that's what happened, why did you wait all this time to come looking for this supposed flash drive?"

Vince waved a hand in dismissal. "You don't need to know the details. Suffice it to say the existence of my brother's journal and the storage device was only brought to our attention a week ago. That flash drive belongs to our family, and we want it back."

"Well, I don't have it," Abbie reiterated.

Vince's upper lip curled. "Sticking to your story, huh? I know you have it, and I'm on my last nerve. Either you give it to me or I'll put a bullet through your boyfriend here."

"He's not my boyfriend," Abbie quickly refuted.

Ethan was surprised to find how deeply the denial cut through him. Regret gave him pause before he quickly pulled his focus back to finding a way out of this untenable situation. "Look, we clearly don't have this drive you're looking for. For all you know, it doesn't even exist. You and I both know that if your business dealings are on the up and up, as you say they are, you wouldn't be resorting to terrorizing an innocent woman. I don't know many upstanding professionals who have hired guns on their payroll or who resort to kidnapping. You're just digging a deeper hole for yourself."

"How I run my operation is none of your business. I want what's mine, and I'll do whatever it takes to get it." Leveling his gun at Ethan's chest, Vince turned to Abbie. "I'm done debating. If you don't want anything happening to your knight in shining armor, you'll turn the flash drive over to me. Now. You've got to the count of three. One…two…"

His gaze tangling with Abbie's, Ethan shook his head urgently. He prayed she would understand his silent plea that she hold her ground and not give in. His heart twisted in his chest when he saw the resolve on her face. She was going to cave to Vince's demands. The next words out of her mouth confirmed her intent.

"Okay," she cried. "I'll give you the drive. I don't have it with me, but I can take you to it."

"Abbie! No!" Ethan protested. His opposition earned him a fierce uppercut to the jaw from Vince's goon.

The force of the violent blow brought him to his knees, but the distraction was exactly the opening he needed. Surreptitiously reaching for his ankle holster, he drew his hidden secondary weapon and lunged at Vince. Placing the snub-nosed revolver against the man's temple, he wrapped an arm around the man's neck and yanked him in front of himself and Abbie like a human shield. "Put your guns down or your boss dies," he barked out, his tone brooking no argument.

Sweat beaded on Vince's upper lip as he hastily snapped out an order to his henchmen. "Do as he says!"

The men were moving to comply when Edgar suddenly emerged from the woods, the rifle in his hands directed squarely at Abbie. "Let my son go if you want her to keep breathing!" he snarled, his dark eyes blazing.

Dismayed at Edgar Romola's unforeseen appearance and the sudden turn the battle had now taken, Ethan hastily weighed his options. If he tried to shoot his way out, Abbie would certainly be hurt in the crossfire...or worse. Conceding defeat, he set his revolver down and raised his hands in surrender.

Edgar pinned him with a menacing glare. "Surprised to see me? I didn't want to get involved, but apparently if I want something done right, I have to do it myself. You and your lady friend have proven to be far more worthy adversaries than I anticipated, but this ends now. I want my flash drive. Hand it over."

"She doesn't have it with her," Vince supplied. "She was about to take us to it when her friend decided to be a hero."

Edgar arched a brow at Abbie. "Okay. Then this is how this is going to go. You're going to take us to where you've stashed that drive. Your game warden friend here is going to hang back until we're gone. If he doesn't come after us, no one will get hurt. I just want what's mine. There's no need for bloodshed."

"I'll take you to it," Abbie promised, her voice breaking. "Just don't hurt Ethan."

"I'm a man of my word. If he upholds his end of the deal, I'll uphold mine. Now, let's get moving." Eyes narrowing to slits, he pinned Ethan with a hard glare. "Everyone but you."

"Do what he says Ethan. Please!" Abbie urged.

Ethan wanted to heed her request. He really did. But he couldn't stand there and watch Edgar and Vince Romola and their goons take the woman who had come to mean the world to him away at gunpoint. Every fiber of his being balked at the idea of standing down. He had to act!

Abbie and the men had begun walking down the path that led to the ocean, toward the boat waiting for them at the shoreline. Intending to strike back cautiously and strategically, he headed for the cover of the trees. Hugging tight to the edge of the woods, he skirted the footpath to avoid detection while he waited for his window of opportunity to make a move.

His progress went unnoticed until his foot accidentally freed a loose patch of shale, sending rock shards skittering noisily down the cliffside. At the noise, Vince spun around and spotted him. Aiming his rifle, he pulled the trigger.

Ethan dived for the ground. He was fast, but not fast enough. The rocketing projectile grazed his shoulder, the force of the hit slamming him to the ground and driving his head against the unyielding rock. His last thought before everything went black was of Abbie.

* * *

Jarred back to consciousness by the raucous cries of seagulls soaring overhead, Ethan gritted his teeth against the fiery inferno blazing in his shoulder and the incessant pounding in his head. His only thought was of Abbie, and the valuable time he'd lost. Rushing to his feet, he tore down the trail. His insides contorted when he spotted her camera lying abandoned on the ground, but he raced on.

Resuming his search, he heard the roar of a speedboat motor over the thunder of the crashing waves. Picking up his pace, he followed the sound to the shoreline, where he saw the vessel in the distance, leaving white foam and churning water in its wake as it hurtled out to sea. The sight was the embodiment of his worst nightmare.

Abbie was on that boat! And he'd arrived too late to save her.

ELEVEN

Held at gunpoint on the speedboat the Romolas had forced her to board, icy fingers of terror clamped around Abbie's heart as she contemplated her odds of escaping. Her abductors were focused on getting to their destination. If they dropped their guard for even a second, she could dive overboard. She was a strong swimmer, and the coastline was less than a mile away.

Despite the very real possibility that her attempt to break free could fail, the move would still buy precious time for Ethan to catch up with her and her captors. If there was even the slightest chance Ethan was alive, she knew he'd come looking for her. But what if he hadn't survived?

Determined to rest in faith and choose hope, she hastily shoved that excruciating thought to the furthest recesses of her mind. She was going to find a way out of this mess. She wasn't going to dwell on her final glimpse of Ethan lying motionless on the ground.

Easier said than done, when the image had seared itself into her brain. The devastating moment when she'd seen Vince turn to shoot Ethan kept replaying on an endless loop. How could he survive that?

Ethan is not dead! she told herself, needing it to be true as urgently as she needed to draw her next breath. He was alive, and he would find the clue she'd left behind for him.

She would not allow herself to consider the very real possibility he might have been fatally injured, because she simply could not keep on going if she'd lost him.

Ethan had brought hope to her life when she'd needed it the most. Her every waking moment after the Spitting Image Slayer's attack had been tainted by memories of the nightmare he'd put her through. If it hadn't been for Ethan, the experience she'd endured would have left her a shell of her former self.

Though there was no point nurturing the hope that she and Ethan might one day have a future together, maybe they could at least be friends. She didn't want to be exiled from him ever again. But first, she had to get out of this alive.

The boat was midway to the shore when a vicious swell tossed it into the air. As it came plummeting back down, Edgar, Vince and their henchmen, and the guns they held trained on her, were pitched off-kilter. Seeing her window of opportunity to escape, she seized the moment.

Holding her breath, Abbie jumped from the vessel. Though it was June, the water was frigid enough to snatch the oxygen from her lungs. The thrum of the boat's engine echoed in her ears as she dived under the surface and swam away. Hoping the choppy waves breaking above her would camouflage her location, she propelled her body toward the shore. It wasn't long before her muscles, numbed by the chilly water, began to tire. Her lungs were screaming for oxygen. She'd have to surface soon.

Praying she'd put enough distance between herself and

her captors, she emerged from the frigid depths, gasping for air. Temporarily blinded by the bright rays of sunlight glinting off the surface of the ocean, it took her a moment to get her bearings.

The Romolas weren't similarly disadvantaged. Her appearance was marked by angry shouts from the boat. Seeing the vessel turning toward her, she took a huge gulp of air and plunged back underwater.

The roar of the speedboat's engine told her the craft was gaining on her quickly. She urged her cold-numbed arms and legs to move faster, but her heavy limbs wouldn't cooperate. With the muscles in her injured leg seizing, she had no option but to surface.

Treading water, she fought against the current to stay afloat. Through eyes blurry from the salty ocean, she saw the speedboat racing toward her. Vince was at the helm, his face twisted in rage, and Edgar had his gun trained on her. Her arms and legs were as heavy as her heart. There was no way she could outswim the vessel. She was once again at the Romola family's mercy.

The speedboat was beside her now. Powerless to defend herself, she surrendered as Edgar ordered one of his henchmen to drag her out of the water.

They deposited her in the boat, and Vince had one of the men take over piloting the craft. She shivered under the Arctic frost of Vince's livid glare.

"Try another stupid trick like that and you'll regret it," he hissed, flexing and unflexing his fists in time with the thrumming of the pulse beat in his jaw.

She saw it now, the same insanity that had swarmed in the black hole of Vito's eyes as he'd stared at her from behind the mask he'd worn the night he abducted her.

Vince Romola, in his current state of unguarded anger, was displaying the same depths of depravity as his twin. Vince was no different than Vito. He was simply more adept at hiding his malicious streak. That made him doubly dangerous.

Drenched and exhausted, she shuddered as she pressed her body back against the boat seat in an effort to put as much distance between herself and Vince as possible.

"There's no running away from your fate, Abbie," Vince taunted, the hardness in his voice jarring her frayed nerves. "You wouldn't be in this position if you'd left well enough alone, but you had to keep poking around, didn't you?"

Edgar glowered at her, his lips set in a bitter line. "Hopefully you've learned a valuable lesson. Fortunately for you, I'm a reasonable man. All you have to do is see your part of our deal through. Return my flash drive, and you'll be free to go."

"You already broke your promise once when you let Vince shoot Ethan. How do I know you won't kill me after I give you what you want?" she challenged.

"You'll have to take my word for it," he sneered.

The expression on his face made her skin crawl. It was pure evil. Engulfed by a wave of defeat that threatened to drown her, she reminded herself she wasn't alone in this battle. She would not allow herself to plunge down that deep, dark abyss of *why me*s. She couldn't go back to that desperate place. If she did, she was afraid those despairing thoughts would suck her in forever. She hadn't given up when faced with untenable horrors before. She would not give up now.

Her break for freedom had been foiled, but it wasn't a

total loss. She'd thrown a monkey wrench in her captors' plans by stalling their progress. If she could find a way to keep them from gaining ground again, she might buy enough time for Ethan to catch up with them.

Right now, she needed to conserve her strength and come up with a plan to delay Vince and his father after they docked. She'd told them she'd hidden the flash drive at the Warden Service's chalet. Her choice of location was a calculated one. She'd seen a flash drive in the laptop on the desk in the basement office when they'd escaped through the tunnel. She would pass that storage device off as the one they were after.

She was well aware her captors weren't stupid. They would check the contents of the drive as soon as they had a chance. But her ploy only had to work long enough to stall them until Ethan arrived.

Mooring the boat, Edgar gave orders to his men. A tremor streaked down Abbie's spine when he turned his attention to her. "An urgent matter has come up that I need to take care of. I'm leaving Vince to handle this situation. His associate, Mark, is going to tag along to make sure you behave yourself. Remember, no more funny business. Vince is going to rent a car, and you're going to direct him and Mark to the chalet where you left my flash drive. I've told them if you make one wrong move, they have my permission to deal with you in whatever manner they see fit."

"Let's go," Vince ordered, the press of the cold, hard metal against her back forcing her to follow his command.

Edgar turned to his son. "Text me with your location when you get there. I'll meet up with you when I'm done here."

Once Vince secured a rental car, Abbie gave him directions to the chalet. Remembering the labyrinth of camp roads on the way, she chose the longest possible route. The strategy was a dicey one. Vince would undoubtedly run out of patience if he figured out she was leading him on a wild goose chase. But she needed every second of precious time her last-ditch tactic would buy if Ethan was going to reach her before it was too late.

She was sure he would find the clue she'd left behind for him. And she was certain when he located her camera and saw the photo of the chalet on its screen he would realize where she was headed and he'd come for her.

Painfully retracing his steps back up the trail, Ethan stopped when he reached Abbie's abandoned camera. He bent to retrieve it, sucking in a breath when the device's LCD screen flickered to life, revealing an image of the Warden Service's chalet. The breath he'd taken snagged in his chest as he realized she must have deliberately cued up the photo to lead him to her. *Clever girl!*

Knowing where she was headed was a game changer. Now, he just needed to get to her before the Romolas figured out she didn't have what they were looking for. First, he needed to phone for backup. He couldn't put Abbie in even more danger by going after the Romolas on his own, no matter how much he wanted to. There was no cell phone service on the island, but he could use Hunter's landline to alert the authorities to Abbie's kidnapping.

Racing to Hunter's house, he rushed inside only to find the phone was dead. The Romolas must have cut the line. Frantic, he ran back outside to the van. He needed to get to a working landline, and Hunter had spoken highly of her closest neighbor. She'd told him Eden was a former FBI agent who'd moved to the island a few months back. If Hunter trusted her, that was good enough for him.

A warm trickle of blood coursed down his arm, reminding him he needed to do something about his injury. Gingerly pulling up his sleeve, he winced when the fabric brushed the deep gouge. Inspecting the wound, he was relieved to find the bullet had only grazed the muscle. The cut was nasty, but the bleeding was gradually beginning to slow. Grabbing the first aid kit from the van, he hastily patched up the gash.

Speeding to Eden's home, he went weak with relief when he pulled into the driveway and saw a black sports car parked there. She was home! Leaping out of the van, he left the vehicle running for Zane and rushed to the front door of a whitewashed Cape similar in design to Hunter's house. Before he had a chance to knock, the door was flung open by a pretty brunette.

"I saw you drive up like the house was on fire," she said, concern flickering in her warm brown eyes. Her gaze widened as she spotted the blood-soaked bandage on his shoulder. "Who are you, and what's going on?"

Ethan showed her his badge. "My name is Ethan Knight. I'm with the Maine Warden Service, and I'm a friend of Hunter's. I'm assisting the NYPD on a case. May I use your phone?"

"Of course! Come in. It's right around the corner on the counter in the kitchen."

"Thank you." Phone in hand, he was about to dial when a chilling thought gave him pause. Who could he call? He still didn't know who was trustworthy. There was a very good chance the Romola family had informants at the Warden Service, the NYPD and possibly even within the local agencies. Still, he couldn't go into this situation without backup.

Seeing his hesitation, Eden walked up, her gaze silently questioning. "Is everything okay?"

With a grim shake of his head, he set the phone down. "I'm not sure calling for backup is a good idea, after all. The NYPD detective I'm assisting is protecting a woman who's been targeted by the mob. We've been safeguarding her here on the island, but he had to leave to chase down a crucial lead in the case. Shortly after, Abbie and I were attacked. She was taken. I know where the men who abducted her are headed, but I can't go after them without reinforcements. Problem is, I don't know who I can trust."

"A leak?" Eden surmised.

"Yeah. Likely more than one. We have reason to believe the people who are after Abbie have contacts in one or more law enforcement agencies. That's a chance I can't take."

"I can provide backup," Eden volunteered without hesitation. "And my former firearms instructor at the FBI is vacationing here. He's staying at an Airbnb on the other side of the island. I can vouch for Landon's trustworthiness. I'm positive he'll want to help."

Ethan scrubbed a hand across his face, his stomach knotted in indecision. If he involved anyone else, he'd be putting their lives at risk. But if he attempted to rescue Abbie solo, there was a chance he could fail. Failure wasn't an option.

"Ethan?" Eden questioned, touching his uninjured arm lightly to pull him from his vacillations.

"Sorry. It's not that I don't appreciate your offer. It's

just that I'm reluctant to drag anyone else into this. One of the men who took Abbie is believed to head up a major crime family. His son is with him, and he is undoubtedly wrapped up in his father's corrupt business dealings, too. These men are dangerous."

She shot him a questioning look. "This man wouldn't happen to be Edgar Romola, would it?"

"Yes," Ethan acknowledged. "You've heard of him, I take it?"

A flicker of pain flashed in her eyes before her eyelids fluttered, shuttering it. Hugging her elbows, she nodded. "He's the reason I'm no longer with the Bureau. Landon is all too familiar with that criminal mastermind, too. When he finds out you're pursuing Edgar, wild horses won't be able to stop him from lending a hand."

"Okay. If you're positive you want to do this, we need to get to the mountains north of here. Abbie left a clue behind to let me know the men who took her are headed to the Warden Service chalet there."

"The ferry leaves in half an hour."

"The ferry is way too slow. Do you have a boat?"

She shook her head. "Just a Jet Ski, but Landon has one."

Ethan paused, considering his next move. Precious seconds were ticking away. If he took the Jet Ski, he could get to Abbie faster. He could send Zane with Eden and Landon on the boat, and they could meet up with him at the chalet. Even a twenty-minute head start might make all the difference.

"I'm assuming Landon travels with a personal sidearm?" he ventured.

"Yes. And I'm licensed to carry, too."

"Good. Do either you or Landon have any experience handling a K-9?"

Eden nodded vigorously. "I'm a private detective now, but I also train K-9s as a sideline. I have two dogs of my own, but I dropped them off on the mainland this morning for their monthly grooming appointment. I'll call and let my groomer know I'm going to be late picking them up. She won't mind taking care of them until I get back."

"Great. My German shepherd, Zane, is in the van. He can accompany you and Landon when you meet me at the rendezvous point."

"Wait. Rendezvous point? You aren't going with us?"

Ethan shook his head. "I'm going to get a head start. That is, if you're willing to let me borrow your Jet Ski, I'll go on ahead of you. You can take Zane, pick up Landon and make the trip by boat. I'll give you directions to the chalet, and I'll make sure there's a rental car waiting for you when you dock."

Eden pursed her lips, unconvinced. "I don't like it. You're injured, and you have no idea what you're going to be walking into. We should go together. There's strength in numbers."

"Normally I would agree. But Edgar Romola is desperate to get his hands on a flash drive, the contents of which we believe could bring him and his entire corrupt empire down. Abbie told him she was taking him to where she's hidden it, but she doesn't have it. It's just a ruse, and I'm terrified of what he'll do to her when he finds out she's bluffing. I have to get to her before he discovers she doesn't have what he wants. If the situation is contained when I arrive, I won't make a move until you and Landon join me. I need backup. I also need to be ready to act before our window of opportunity to rescue her slams shut. For Abbie to have the best shot at surviving this, the sooner help is on the way, the better."

Nodding, she headed for the kitchen. Opening a drawer, she handed him a key. "The Jet Ski is moored at my dock. Follow the set of stairs behind the house. I'll pick up Landon, and we'll be right behind you with your dog. If the situation is contained when you get there, don't make a move until we arrive to back you up.

"I'm still not convinced it's a good idea for you to head there solo, but I can tell you've got your mind made up. It's also plain to see this is personal for you, and I have a hunch that's because of Abbie. Just remember to proceed with your head, not your heart. There's no margin for error."

Ethan didn't bother to deny her speculation. "Thank you. I'll be careful. Before I leave, you should meet Zane."

They stepped outside, and Ethan opened the van door and snapped Zane's lead onto his collar. Leading him out of the van, he commanded him to sit before making the introductions.

"Zane, this is Eden. She and her friend are going to take you on a boat ride."

Immediately clocking the words *boat* and *ride*, the smart-as-a-whip German shepherd whined eagerly, his gaze skipping to Eden.

Ethan passed Zane's lead to Eden, along with a dog treat.

"Aren't you handsome," Eden praised the dog, offering him the biscuit. With a soft woof, Zane gently took the treat. She stroked his chest, and he promptly plopped down at her feet for a belly rub. His broad doggie grin, coupled with Eden's assuredness around the K-9, gave Ethan confidence in his decision to let her look after his partner.

"I'll take good care of him," Eden promised.

"Thank you. I know you will." Retrieving Zane's bulletproof vest from his gear, Ethan secured it around his partner. "He responds to all the standard German commands. Be careful when you get to the rendezvous point. If you see anything out of the ordinary, I want you to stand down."

"I can't promise that," she told him solemnly. "Just because I don't work for the FBI any longer, that doesn't mean I've abandoned my call to serve and protect. But I will be careful."

With no time to argue, Ethan grabbed his gear and said goodbye to Eden and Zane.

Soon he was darting across the ocean on the Jet Ski, putting every ounce of his energy into making up for lost time. Arriving at his destination, he docked the craft and hastily made arrangements for two rental cars, one for him and one for Eden and Landon to collect when they arrived.

After programming the directions to the Warden Service chalet into the second rental car's GPS system, he hit the road. Pushing the vehicle to its limit, he ate up the miles separating him from Abbie. He spent the entire drive praying God would keep her safe and that He'd allow him to arrive in time to prevent the Romolas from harming her.

Nearing the turnoff, he parked the rental car on the side of the road. He'd left a note for Eden in Landon in their rental car with the make and model of his vehicle.

When the pair caught up with him, they'd see his car and know they were close. Traveling the rest of the way on foot would ensure he retained the element of surprise.

As he silently approached the chalet from the rear, the sound of raised voices drifted to him. He couldn't see anyone yet, but the voices were coming from the front of the house. Vince was arguing with a woman, but the husky tenor of her voice told him that woman wasn't Abbie. Had another warden stopped by the chalet and stumbled across the Romolas? If so, where was Abbie?

Heart pounding, he scooted closer, ducking low and hugging the chalet's foundation for cover. Peering around the side of the house, he sagged in relief when he saw Abbie, seemingly unharmed, sandwiched between Vince and one of his henchmen. But where was Edgar?

Vince and his associate were no longer armed. Their weapons lay on the ground in front of a tall blonde woman who had her rifle aimed at the group. It was clear she had taken charge. Had Edgar fled?

The change in dynamics was to his advantage. He'd take that win. Now, he just needed to formulate a plan to deal with the rogue player in the mix. Who was she, and what was her beef with the Romolas?

He could shoot the mystery riflewoman who had Vince, his henchman and Abbie in her sights, but that would be a chancy move with the snub-nosed revolver that was his only weapon at the moment. Beyond the difficulty of making an accurate shot at this distance, there was also the chance that, even if he was successful in incapacitating the mystery woman, Vince and his helper could seize the opportunity to try and reclaim their weapons. Abbie was still far too close to them for Ethan to take that risk.

Eden, Landon and Zane would be here soon. If the coup playing out in front of him didn't turn into a massacre before they arrived, they could still win this war. All he had to do was hold his position and pray the new combatant in this battle wouldn't hurt Abbie.

Catching a glimpse of movement through the trees, he froze. A huge buck sporting a massive rack was heading for a clearing just ahead of him. Ethan's pulse rate accelerated as the animal stepped out of the forest and stood at the edge of the tree line.

The buck's appearance was an unexpected complication. The deer was certain to catch his scent. The animal's reaction would betray his hiding spot, jeopardizing his rescue mission.

The thought of Abbie's captors being alerted to his presence sent trickles of sweat running down his back. Crouching lower, he prayed the buck wouldn't register his scent. As he watched tensely, the buck tossed his head and sniffed the air. Ears swiveling and nose twitching, the big deer blew an angry breath. With another loud snort, he bounded back into the woods, his tail raised like a white flag.

The woman holding the rifle whipped around, her attention captured by the departing deer.

"Ethan. I had a feeling you'd show up," she sniggered. "Unless you want me to put a bullet through your sweet photographer friend here, you'll drop your gun and come and join us."

The woman knew him? Perplexed, Ethan scrutinized her intently. He didn't recognize her stern features, but there was something incredibly familiar about her voice and the cadence of her speech. Her mannerisms struck a familiar chord, as well. He might not remember her, but she obviously knew him. If this wasn't the first time their paths had crossed, maybe he could use that to his advantage.

He was contemplating his next move when the mystery woman fired a warning shot above his head, sending a clear message that she had no tolerance for his vacillation.

"In case you thought that was a suggestion, let me clarify. It isn't a request, it's an order," she ground out. Yanking the bolt back on the rifle, she chambered another round and fired in his direction again. Closer this time. "Last chance."

With no choice but to comply, he set his gun down and joined the group of hostages.

"Ethan!" Abbie cried out. "Are you okay?"

"I'm fine," he assured her. "Are you?"

Nodding, she brushed away a tear. He wanted to run to her and sweep her into his arms, but he couldn't let the woman holding them at gunpoint see how much Abbie meant to him. Their assailant held all the cards, and if she figured out Abbie was important to him, that would only decrease his chances of rescuing her. And he was going to rescue her if it was the last thing he did.

He still didn't know how the woman holding them at gunpoint knew him. He couldn't shake the feeling that he knew her, too. There was something about the resolute set of her shoulders and the way she brandished the weapon that was distinctly familiar. When she flipped a lock of her hair behind her ears, it hit him. He'd seen that identical mannerism hundreds of times before. His stomach bottomed out. Facial reconstruction and blond hair dye might have altered her physical appearance, but the outward transformation hadn't changed her personality traits. Traits he knew all too well.

"Gabriella?" he gasped.

TWELVE

Gabriella aimed the rifle toward Ethan's chest. "It's Winona now," she corrected matter-of-factly. "I didn't think you'd recognize me. I'm touched. I guess I meant more to you than I realized."

Grappling to wrap his mind around the surreal situation, Ethan could only stare. This woman standing here holding a gun on him looked nothing like the vivacious brunette he'd worked alongside for years—the partner whose death he had mourned. She wasn't the same woman whose back he'd once covered, and who he'd trusted to cover his. Gabriella—no, Winona, he amended—had changed.

"I thought you were dead," he choked out, his voice thick with disbelief.

"That was the whole idea," she huffed impatiently, as though the reason for her unfathomable act should be obvious to him. "I needed to end my old existence and start a new one. Faking my death was the only way."

"But why?" he pressed, needing to know what had prompted her to do something so rash. "I don't understand. This isn't who you are."

Winona waved off his remonstration. "Oh, but it is. My

old life was all one big lie. On her deathbed, my mother told me my father hadn't passed away before I was born like she'd led me to believe. Truth was, she'd gotten involved with a wealthy businessman. When he learned she was pregnant, he paid her to 'take care of things' and pretend nothing had ever happened between them. She went along with it, only she couldn't bring herself to end the pregnancy. And she never dared to tell him about me because she knew that would be the end of both of us. My real father is Edgar Romola."

"You're Edgar's daughter?" Ethan blurted.

"Shocking, right? At first, I didn't know what to think. Little by little, it all began to make sense. No wonder I'd always felt like an outsider. I'd spent my whole life alone, never feeling like I belonged. My mother was always so busy trying to keep a roof over our heads and food on our plates that I was with sitters more than I was with her. Now I have a family. Someplace to belong. A birthright! I want to take my rightful place in my new family."

Abbie gaped at the woman. "And your idea of joining the family means standing here holding a gun on us and your half brother?"

Tossing her head in Vince's direction, Winona sneered. "Vince still doesn't trust me. Neither does my father. Even though I agreed to a DNA test—a test that proved I was telling the truth—they're still in denial. They don't believe I won't betray them."

"But you managed to convince Vito you were trustworthy, didn't you?" Ethan ventured.

"He's the only one who would even acknowledge me," she replied, her voice laced with hurt. "Because I was a detective for the NYPD, Edgar and Vince were convinced

I was trying to worm my way into the family so I could entrap them. They thought I was more loyal to the badge than to blood. Can you believe it? My own father thought I was playing him, trying to prove he was a criminal.

"I decided to change my approach and focus on getting close to Vito. I tailed him one night, hoping to get a chance to talk to him. That's when I saw him abduct a woman. I continued tailing him and he led me to where he had another woman bound to a tree. That's when I realized he was the Spitting Image Slayer. I confronted him, promising to keep his secret if he would help me convince our father I was sincere in wanting to be a part of the family and that I didn't have a hidden agenda."

Ethan shot her a withering glare. "You took an oath to serve and protect. How could you cover up Vito's crimes?" he prodded. He needed to keep her talking. The longer she was distracted, the greater the chance Eden and Landon would arrive in time. "How could you turn your back on the career you loved and that you'd worked so hard for?"

Rolling her eyes, Winona impatiently waved away his words. "Your heart was in the job. Mine never was. When I discovered I was Edgar's daughter, I knew I'd found where I really belonged."

"If you wanted to throw your life away by turning your back on everything you'd sworn to uphold, then why not simply resign as a detective and join Edgar without going to the extreme of staging your own death?" Ethan demanded.

"My connection to the NYPD was a liability. Edgar values total devotion above all else. Simply resigning from the force was never going to be enough to convince him I could be trusted. I'd put some of his contemporaries behind bars. I'd fought to suppress the very things his empire was built on. I couldn't just walk away from the job. I had to make all my ties to law enforcement disappear. To do that, I had to disappear Gabriella Fernandez and reinvent myself."

Ethan clenched his fists, his nostrils flaring. "So you deceived everyone into thinking you'd been brutally murdered?"

Winona shrugged. "Yes. To exchange the lie of a life I was leading so I could be welcomed where I truly belonged. My father demands total devotion from his associates. Even more so from blood. I had to do something drastic in order to make him see I was worthy of his trust. I decided to fake my death and assuming a new identity, and Vito offered to help. Making it look like I was a victim of the Spitting Image Slayer was his idea. All I had to do was make sure you were on hand to witness our little performance.

"When Vito pushed me into the river after he pretended to stab me, I swam to a boat he had waiting. He'd prepared everything I needed to assume my new identity. The last step was a bit of facial reconstruction work and a change of hair color and style. Just like that, Gabriella ceased to exist and Winona was born."

Incredulous, Ethan shook his head. "You were a valued member of the NYPD family. What about your career and your friends that you left behind? Didn't the people who cared about you mean anything to you?"

Winona pursed her lips. "No one cared about Gabriella Fernandez. As for the career I left behind, every time I put on that NYPD badge I was putting my life on the line. The majority of the people we were working to protect respected us less than the criminals we were trying to keep them safe from. You were the only one there who treated me with decency."

"Sure, there were tough days," Ethan acknowledged. "But you were making a difference. The work you did mattered. Every criminal we took off the street was a win."

Winona laughed harshly. "Come on. You don't really buy that, do you? If you did, you'd still be wearing a shield instead of policing wildlife in the middle of nowhere."

Ethan felt the blood drain from his face as her words hit home. "I admit that I ran from the job. Part of the reason is because I thought I'd failed you. I've carried a ton of guilt ever since that night. I was convinced I could have done something differently to change the outcome."

The *if only*s had nearly destroyed him.

"You're such a Boy Scout," Winona dismissed, rolling her eyes. "But that's so you. Always making sacrifices for the greater good."

"I can live with that as my legacy. Will you be able to live with the fallout from the bad decisions you've made trying to gain your father's approval—approval that might always remain out of reach?"

"It's not out of reach," she barked out, the expression in her cold, hard eyes driving home her belief in the declaration. "And where did living by the rules get me? I've found the real me now. As Winona Romola, I'm going to leave my mark on this world. I'm going to gain my father's trust by getting the flash drive he's after." She turned to Vince. "Thank you for doing all the legwork to locate it, by the way. You made things so much easier by leading me to Abbie."

Her assertion only infuriated Vince further. His face flamed as he fisted his hands at his side. "What are you planning to do with it?"

"I'm going to take the credit for retrieving it, of course. But this time I'm going to hold on to it as my insurance policy. It's my key to the Romola kingdom. When our father sees I'm protecting his interests and not leveraging the information to get him thrown in prison, he'll beg me to join the family."

Ethan's lips thinned in a grim line. "Do you really believe that? You've seen what men like him are capable of. They're loyal to no one."

"Family should accept you unconditionally," Abbie added softly. "If you have to hold something over their heads to get them to let you close, something's wrong."

Winona's face fell. "My father is just being cautious. I understand why he needs me to demonstrate my loyalty. I'll do whatever it takes to prove my devotion to him and the family."

"It's going to take a lot more than that to make him accept you into his family," Ethan asserted.

Nostrils flaring, Winona waved the rifle in his direction. "Now you're making me wish I'd shot you and your photographer friend when I eliminated Vito. I don't know why I caved into my soft spot for you and let you live."

Ethan sucked in a shocked breath. "*You* shot Vito?"

Winona's upper lip curled. "He had to be dealt with. Vito was with Edgar when our father reluctantly agreed to a meeting to talk, after I'd first learned I was his daughter. The meeting was a bust. Afterward, Vito invited me to his penthouse. He told me I should give up trying to win Edgar over—that it was never going to happen.

"Of course, I told him I had no intention of doing any such thing. That's when he completely lost it, ranting about how I was trying to take his place. He stormed out in such a rage that he forgot he was leaving me alone in his penthouse. I took advantage of the opportunity to poke around, hoping I might come across something that would help me learn more about our father. Instead, I found Vito's journal and discovered he intended to double-cross the family."

Ethan clenched his fists. "You murdered him. Nothing justifies what you did."

"He *had* to die," Winona spat venomously. "He'd devised an elaborate plan to undermine our father and take control of the family business. He'd outlined every step of his scheme in his journal. He was going to pretend to carry out our father's orders to end Abbie. He planned to attack her, but he didn't plan on finishing the job. He needed her to live so she would find the flash drive he left with her with evidence of Edgar's drug deals and money laundering. He knew she'd find an expert who could crack the encryption, and then use the information on the drive to expose my family's criminal ventures.

"He wanted to destroy our father, but he didn't want to chance the betrayal being traced back to him if he turned the evidence in anonymously to the police or the media, since Edgar has so many people in his pocket. I had to stop him, so I put a counterplan in play. I went to the scene and hid on the sidelines. When Vito showed up, that's when I called you, Ethan, so you would catch him in the act."

"*You* were behind the anonymous call I got that night?" Ethan stammered, incredulous.

She nodded. "I made the call using a voice-changer device. I wanted you to capture Vito and charge him for his crimes as the Spitting Image Slayer. But as I was waiting I realized that, even behind bars, Vito was too great a threat to our father alive. He knew too much. I had to make sure he would never be a menace to our family again, so I shot him. Afterward, I went to the hospital and posed as a nurse so I could retrieve the flash drive from Abbie's personal belongings. Once I found it tucked in her jacket pocket, I contacted Edgar and made arrangements to meet him. I brought him Vito's journal, along with the drive, so he'd understand why Vito had to die."

"And he was grateful," Vince spat in utter incredulity. "You killed his son—my twin brother—and he thanked you for it!"

"Yes. Because he understood that Vito's goal had been to destroy him. Mark here is glad I took Vito out, too, I'll bet. Aren't you, Mark?"

Eyes darting between Vince and Winona, the man remained silent.

Winona sighed. "It's so hard to get good help these days."

Before Ethan could voice the question that was on the tip of his tongue, Abbie spoke up.

"I don't understand. You gave the flash drive to your father. You must *know* I don't have it. Why are you asking me for it?" she demanded.

"There's a copy," Vince grated out. "We only recently learned of the second drive. Vito was incredibly paranoid, though, so it fits. He left a failsafe so if someone other than you got ahold of the first flash drive, his plan would still work. When Gabriella—Winona," he corrected, "gave my father the flash drive, Edgar set it aside, thinking it was just another one of her attempts to worm her way into his good graces.

"A couple of weeks ago, he happened upon the flash drive and decided to see what was on it. It was password protected and encrypted, so he enlisted the help of one of his most trusted associates. When the man cracked the algorithm and gained access to the drive, he found hundreds of files. Combing through them, he noticed duplication flags that clued him in to the existence of a copy."

"Vito never mentioned a second flash drive in his journal," Winona mused. "I didn't know it existed until Edgar called to ask if I had it. I didn't, but I promised to get it for him. He said if I delivered, he'd welcome me with open arms."

"Ha!" Vince scoffed. "Some way to try and join the family. You murdered my brother, and now you're holding a gun on me? My father considered Vito disposable, but I can assure you he values me. He sent *me* to retrieve the drive. You should be helping me, not holding me at gunpoint. Let me go, and I'll get Abbie to turn the second flash drive over to me. Then we can bring it to our father together."

Winona stared at her half brother incredulously. "Do you think I'm an idiot? Suddenly we're on the same side, when up until now you've refused to acknowledge we share the same father? You want to open your arms to me after you shut me out just like Vito did? How convenient." She tossed her head. "I don't think so.

"I'm in charge now, and here's how things are going

to go down. Ethan, you're going to take those handcuffs you're carrying and you're going to shackle Vince and Mark to that tree over there. Then, you're going to tag along while Abbie takes me to where she's hidden my father's flash drive. That way, if she changes her mind and decides not to cooperate, you're going to be the one who pays the price." Swinging her rifle pointedly toward Ethan, she jerked the barrel to emphasize her statement.

Abbie took a step forward. "Ethan isn't involved in this. Leave him alone! I'll give you what you want."

Ethan's breath hitched in his chest as Abbie's gaze locked with his. She no longer appeared frightened. She was looking at him as though his mere presence guaranteed that everything was going to be just fine. He was humbled by her faith in him. He certainly didn't deserve it. And there was no way he was worthy of her love.

Love. Every beat of his heart pounded out the message that it was time for him to stop running from the emotion—to stop running from what he felt for her. Because, no matter how hard he'd tried to convince himself otherwise, he could no longer deny he loved her.

God had brought this special woman into his life, and he'd been afraid to trust that she was different from Sondra. He'd ghosted Abbie, pushing her away because he'd been terrified if he let her get close she would hurt him like Sondra had. But Abbie wasn't Sondra.

Abbie hadn't simply challenged his vow never to let another woman into his heart again, she'd obliterated all the emotional defense mechanisms he'd put in place to ensure he upheld that vow.

He'd wasted far too much precious time letting his fear of putting his heart on the line keep him from the happiness he and Abbie were meant to share. He was done running. The first thing he was going to do when he extracted them from this predicament was tell her he loved her.

"I don't have all day, Ethan," Winona grumbled, pulling him from his musings. "Now, get moving. The quicker I have that flash drive in hand, the sooner this will be over."

Shifting to comply with the order, Ethan spotted a flash of movement out of the corner of his eye. He turned in time to see Mark whip a throwing star from his waistband. A second later, the man sent the weapon rocketing toward Winona.

Winona ducked to evade the throwing star flying in her direction, but she wasn't fast enough to avoid the speeding blade. The weapon collided with her shoulder, and she dropped to her knees, shrieking as the sharp tips embedded in her skin. Instantly, Mark and Vince bolted for her, intent on disarming her.

Seizing the distraction, Ethan grabbed Abbie's hand. "Run!" he cried out.

Heart hammering, Abbie darted into the cover of the forest alongside Ethan. Terror gripped her as harrowing memories of her futile attempt to run from Vito the night he'd abducted her came flooding back. She couldn't let Vince catch them!

Forcing herself to push past the pain shooting through her weak leg, she kept pace with Ethan as he tore through the forest, his hand clasped tightly around hers. She was already as exhausted as if she'd run a marathon, yet they'd only covered a short distance. Muscles screaming in agony, she paused, taking deep gulps of air as she massaged the burning tendons in her thigh, hating that she was slowing him down.

"We have to keep moving. We're almost there," he encouraged. "Let me carry you."

"That would slow us down even more," she panted, gulping air to fuel her oxygen-starved lungs. "I can do this," she insisted, determined to keep going.

Fueled by desperation, she pressed on. When she grew tired again, Ethan insisted she lean on him for support. Just when she was certain she couldn't take another step, he came to an abrupt halt.

Looking up, she realized they'd reached the mouth of the tunnel they'd exited earlier to board the helicopter.

Pushing aside a large stone, Ethan revealed a concealed keypad and quickly entered a code. "You'll be safe here," he assured her, steering her inside as soon as the door slid open.

"Me?" she blurted, freezing on the threshold as the intent behind his words sank in. "What about you? Aren't you coming?"

He shook his head, his face an unreadable mask. "I'm going to create a diversion. Backup is on the way. I just need to hold them off until help arrives."

"No! It's too dangerous. And you're hurt."

Ethan's eyes flicked to the makeshift bandage he'd wrapped around his shoulder wound. "This? It's just a scratch," he assured her with an unconcerned grin. "Wait for me here. I'll be back before you know it."

Opening her mouth to debate his instructions, Abbie was astounded when he leaned in and kissed her. The tender brush of his warm lips against hers overflowed with promise—a promise that felt like the future she longed to share with him.

She froze for a moment, stunned, not daring to believe the moment was real. A surge of yearning, sharp and sweet, coursed through her. Even if this was all just a dreamy hallucination, she was going to make the most of the fantasy. Melting into him, she poured all the love in her heart into the merging of their lips.

When Ethan broke off the kiss, he continued to hold her in his arms. Cradling her close, he pressed his mouth tenderly to her forehead before releasing her and stepping away. His dazed smile told her the kiss they'd shared had left him as thunderstruck as it had her.

"I promise I'll be back for you," he vowed resolutely.

A deluge of emotions washed over her—elation, hope, fear for the situation they were embroiled in and concern for Ethan's safety as he risked everything for her— No, she amended, as she watched him head for the door. He wasn't just risking everything for her. He was risking everything for *them.*

Struck with wonder by this rush of feelings too new and too joyous for her to even begin to wrap her mind around, she stood there speechless as Ethan turned and waved goodbye before pulling the door shut behind him.

The metallic click of the lock engaging roused her from her shock. Ethan cared about her. The knowledge drove her into action. If he thought she was going to stay tucked away in the safety of this tunnel while he put his life on the line for her, he was mistaken. She wasn't going to let him risk everything while she sat here, insulated from danger. They were meant to be a team, and she fully intended to do her part.

Vince and Winona both wanted the flash drive they thought she had. She was going to make sure they got it, albeit in the form of a decoy. She'd brought them here because she'd seen a flash drive in a laptop in the basement office. Vince and Winona wouldn't have a way to verify the flash drive was the genuine article until they got to a computer. All she had to do was secure it and then hide the laptop in the tunnel where the Romolas couldn't find it.

Beseeching God to keep Ethan safe, she headed for the chalet entrance at the other end of the tunnel. The muscles in her overworked and still-recovering leg trembled with fatigue, but she pressed forward. Reaching the trapdoor, she cautiously pushed it open.

Peering up the stairs that led out of the tunnel, she saw the basement office was empty. Upstairs, all was silent. The laptop with the flash drive she intended to hand off to the Romolas was on the desk.

Climbing the stairs out of the tunnel, she entered the office and rushed to the computer. After transferring the files on the flash drive to a folder on the laptop, she erased the storage device. Then she affixed a password to ensure that, on the off chance the Romolas were able to secure access to another computer, they wouldn't immediately discover they'd been duped.

Removing the flash drive from its port, she scooped the laptop up and descended the stairs to the tunnel, where she hid the computer safely away.

Satisfied her plan would buy them time if Ethan did run into trouble, she made her way back up to the office. Closing the door to the tunnel, she pulled the rug into place, making sure the hidden entrance was completely concealed.

Now, all she could do was wait for Ethan to return. Technically, he'd told her to stay in the tunnel. But if she obeyed, she wouldn't be able to see or hear anything. She wouldn't know if he needed help. He'd probably be upset with her for not listening to him, but she had to do something.

The crack of a pistol firing outside had her heart leaping to her throat. *God, don't let Ethan be hurt.* An involuntary shiver zipped down her spine as she rushed upstairs. Scooting down out of sight, she headed for the window closest to where the shot had rung out. Peeking out, her eyes widened in horror as she spotted Ethan struggling to gain control of Vince's handgun.

Punches flying, the men grappled furiously. Both had their hands on the gun as they wrestled. They stopped abruptly when they smacked into the trunk of a huge pine tree. The impact jostled the weapon from their grip, sending it soaring through the air to land a few feet away.

The men were scrambling to reach the gun when the deep boom of a rifle shot pierced the air. A moment later, the shooter materialized from the trees. *Winona!*

Ignoring the excruciating pain in her injured leg, Abbie ran for the front door of the chalet. She had to stop Winona before she hurt Ethan! She'd use the flash drive to bargain for his safety.

Palms sweaty with fear, Abbie eased the door open a crack and saw Winona level her rifle at the warring men.

"That's enough!" Winona barked out. "Stand up this instant and step away from the gun."

With no alternative other than to do as she'd ordered, Ethan and Vince complied.

Spotting his associate's white shirt wrapped around Winona's shoulder wound, Vince's face reddened in rage. "Where's Mark? What did you do to him?" he demanded.

"Relax," Winona leered. "I didn't kill him. I only knocked him unconscious. Now, I've lost my patience, and I've had it with these ridiculous games. Where's Abbie?"

Abbie's stomach roiled at the vitriol lacing the woman's voice, but she didn't let it sway her from what she knew she had to do. Steeled by her resolve to save Ethan, she stepped out of the chalet into Winona's line of sight. "I'm right here!" she called out, holding up the flash drive. "I've got what you want. I'll give it to you, but not until you release Ethan and promise you won't kill us."

Winona's eyes slanted menacingly. "Trying to bargain from a position of weakness is a bold move."

Muscles quivering, Abbie shrugged, striving to appear nonchalant. "Not so bold. I have the flash drive you're looking for," she disputed evenly.

"There's nothing stopping me from shooting you and taking it." Winona retorted menacingly.

Balling her shaking hands into fists to hide her trembling fingers, Abbie fought to keep her voice steady. "That's where you're wrong," she asserted, digging deep to find the boldness she needed to convey. Holding up an index card and a lighter, she set the paper aflame. "That's the password for the drive going up in smoke. I have it memorized. I'll give you the flash drive as soon as you let Ethan walk here to me. When he's safe, I'll tell you thc password."

Winona's eyebrows furrowed, her eyes flashing with fury. "How do I know you'll give me the real password and not a fake? I can't verify it until I plug the drive into a computer."

Abbie met the woman's cold, hard gaze squarely. "You're going to have to trust me, just like I'm going to have to trust you to let Ethan and me go free. We're both taking a leap of faith, but that's the only way to ensure you and I both get what we want. Do we have a deal?"

A bead of sweat trickled down Abbie's back, the deafening jackhammering of her pulse in her ears the only noise to punctuate the hear-a-pin-drop silence hanging thick in the air as Winona stared her down. She kept her gaze steady, refusing to back down.

Backed into a corner, Winona had no alternative but to cave. "Deal," she agreed.

Abbie's fingers were damp as she lobbed the flash drive in Winona's direction. Holding her breath as the woman dived for the prize, her eyes darted to Ethan as he raced toward her. Every step he took brought him closer to her and farther away from danger.

The instant Ethan reached her, he stepped in front of her to shield her. "The password is DoubleJeopardy," she called out to Winona, feeling behind her for the doorknob and turning it. "It's all one word. The *D* and the *J* are capitalized."

Not waiting for a response, she scooted into the house. Ethan followed her inside, locking the door behind them.

"Head for the tunnel," he instructed.

The instant they were secure in the secret room, he wrapped his arms around her in a hug born of both relief and joy. "You were brilliant," he praised, holding her tightly. "Are you sure you weren't meant to have a career in law enforcement?"

"Positive." She grinned, hugging him back fiercely. "Not a fan of being shot at, remember? How much longer before the backup you're expecting arrives?"

Before he could reply, the creak of the trapdoor opening sounded above them. Spinning around, they saw Mark standing at the top of the stairs, his chest bare and his head bloody.

His face a mask of pure evil, he leveled his gun at them. "The help you're expecting won't be here soon enough," he snarled.

THIRTEEN

Mark's lips twisted in a sneer. "The hidden exit is a nice touch. Very tricky. When I broke in, thinking I'd have you trapped, I found the place empty. I knew there was no way you could have slipped past me. When I noticed the bunched-up rug in the basement, I looked under it, and there was the key to your disappearing act. A trapdoor."

Ethan's eyes blazed with fury. "Well, if you're looking for the flash drive, you're too late. Winona has it."

Mark swiped away a trickle of blood that had dripped onto his face from the gash on his head. An angry knot had welled near his temple. "That doesn't mean you're off the hook. Vince and Winona think the flash drive you handed over is the real deal, but I'm not as trusting as they are. I want proof. Until I have it, I'm not letting you out of my sight. Now, follow me!"

Ethan flexed his hands, considering his next move. Although Mark was armed and he wasn't, he'd have the element of surprise on his side if he tackled the man. But while he might be able to overpower the goon, the chance the man's gun might go off in the struggle was too great a risk to take. He couldn't hazard Abbie taking a hit from a stray bullet.

Nodding at her subtly, he silently communicated his intent to play along with Mark. Taking the lead, he began to climb the stairs, all the while racking his brain for another way to extract her safely from this mess.

Keeping his gun trained on them as he stepped backward up the stairs, Mark waited until they'd reached the next-to-the-last tread before backing into the finished basement. Before he had a chance to turn around, a feminine voice rang out, breaking the tense silence.

"Fass!" Eden ordered Zane.

At her command, the K-9 lunged for Mark, a blur of pounding paws and flexing muscles. Snarling menacingly, he clamped his jaws down on the man's gun arm, shaking it until he lost his grip on the weapon. Mark howled in pain as the German shepherd dragged him to the ground and pinned him there.

"Brav! Good job, Zane!" Ethan praised his partner, never so happy to see him as in this moment. After securing the gun Mark had dropped, he handcuffed him and gave his K-9 the command to release the screaming man. Pulling the goon to his feet, he snapped a second set of handcuffs onto the wrist of the man's uninjured arm and secured the other side of the cuffs to a heavy iron radiator.

"Are you guys okay?" Eden blurted in a worried rush.

Ethan nodded. "We're fine, thanks to you. That was great timing! Where's Landon? Is he dealing with the others?"

She shook her head, paling at the mention of her friend's name. "Landon isn't with me. When I got to his vacation rental, I found him unconscious on the living room floor. His place had been trashed and he'd been badly beaten. Burglars have been targeting summer rentals. He must have walked in on a break-in. I called emergency services, and as soon as I knew he was going to be okay, I rushed here. I couldn't leave you to deal with Edgar alone. Zane alerted at the chalet door as soon as we arrived, so I focused on gaining entry to the house. I didn't see anyone else outside."

"Abbie, this is Hunter's friend Eden," Ethan quickly introduced.

Abbie shot her a grateful smile. "Thanks for coming to help. I'm sorry your friend was hurt."

Eden offered a tremulous smile. "Fortunately, I found him in time. If Ethan hadn't stopped and asked for help, I never would have known Landon was in trouble."

Shoulders squared, his eyes filled with gratitude, Ethan met Eden's gaze. "You got us out of a tight spot, showing up when you did."

"Happy to assist," Eden smiled. "It's about time the Romola family answers for their crimes. Speaking of which, where's their patriarch?"

The pulse along Ethan's jaw twitched. "Unfortunately, I don't know. Edgar tasked his associate Mark here and his son, Vince, to deal with retrieving the flash drive. Vince is still on the loose, and there's another player in the mix out there—Edgar has a daughter, and she's after the flash drive, too. I thought Vito killed my NYPD partner, but it turns out it was all a ruse. She staged her death to gain her father's trust. She assumed a new identity and goes by Winona now."

Eden's mouth pursed in surprise at the new information. "Sounds like I got here just in time. We still have work to do."

"Yeah," Ethan agreed. "And this guy is going to help us with that. Aren't you, Mark?"

"In your dreams," the man spat, shooting daggers at Ethan.

Striding over to where he'd left Mark tied up, Ethan checked the bite wound Zane had inflicted. "Between your head injury and that laceration to your arm, the sooner you get medical attention, the better off you'll be. I'll call 911, but first you're going to help me. I want you to call Vince and tell him you have the flash drive. You're going to ask him to come to the chalet."

Mark raised one eyebrow contemptuously. "Why would I do anything for you?"

"Maybe because you'd like to keep the use of your arm? That's a serious bite. I wish I could tell you my K-9's mouth is clean, but oral hygiene isn't his strong suit. I'd hate to see you get a nasty infection. I'm sure you wouldn't want to jeopardize your health because you were too stubborn to do me a simple favor."

"You can't refuse me medical care. I have rights," Mark protested, his eyes blazing with defiance.

"I wouldn't dream of keeping you from getting the help you need. I can take my sweet time making the call for an ambulance, though. How quickly I get emergency services here is up to you. The sooner you get me in touch with Vince, the sooner you'll get the medical attention you need. All you have to do is call your boss, tell him you've got the flash drive and that Gabriella—Winona," he corrected, "attacked you and you need help finding her."

"That's not going to be possible," Mark ground out. "I captured Vince and Winona before I came after you. They were so busy arguing they never even saw me coming. I tied them up and locked them in the cabin of Winona's boat. I'm tired of being low man on the totem pole. Vince bungled the job he was sent to do. Winona is just as incompetent as he is. I'm going to be the one to hand Edgar the flash drive. It's time I get the recognition I deserve for the role I play in this organization."

"Okay, then," Ethan pivoted. "Change of plans. You're going to call Edgar instead."

"Ha! You think I'm crazy? You want me to set Edgar Romola up? No way am I doing that! The moment he figures out I led him into a trap, I'm done for. He'll kill me."

Ethan shrugged. "It's your choice. Just keep in mind the longer you drag your feet, the greater the chance that wound on your arm is going to get infected. For your sake, I hope you're left-handed."

Enraged, Mark's gaze collided with his, challenging him to a staredown. Ethan kept his eyes locked on him, his intensity unwavering.

Tense moments passed, and sweat began to bead on Mark's forehead. "Okay," he caved. "I'll do it."

"Good call," Ethan affirmed. Taking the man's satellite phone from his belt, he started to pass it to him when a loud *whup-whup-whup* reverberated above them.

"A helicopter!" Abbie exclaimed.

Mark upper lip curled. "No need to contact Edgar, after all. He's here. He had Vince text him so he could meet us when he wrapped up some business he had to take care of. Guess he's done."

Resolve sparked in Abbie's eyes. "We can take the tunnel to the landing pad and catch him by surprise," she blurted, her voice a breathless rush.

Gently placing his hand on her arm, Ethan brought

her to a halt as she headed for the basement door. "Not *we*. I need you to hang back here. I can't risk something happening to you. Eden and I have got this. Zane, Pass auf!" he told his K-9, commanding him to stay and keep watch over Abbie and guard Mark.

Indignant, Abbie glared at him. "Oh, no, you don't. I have just as much at stake in this fight as you do. I'm going with you. What if Edgar brought reinforcements? I can use Mark's gun and help even the odds if you find yourselves outnumbered."

"She has a point," Eden inserted. "In any case, we can't stand here debating, or we'll be too late to leverage the element of surprise."

Reluctantly capitulating, Ethan nodded. "Okay, but stay behind Eden and me." Turning to Mark, he glared at the man. "I'm going to leave Zane here to make sure you don't get any ideas about trying to escape."

Pushing open the tunnel door, Ethan surveyed the area. The helicopter was sitting on the landing pad. Although its rotors were still spinning, there was no sign of the pilot or Edgar.

Cautiously inching forward, he took one step and then another. Out of nowhere, a smoke grenade came hurtling toward him. His gut twisted. "They've spotted us! Get down!" he urged.

With a pop and a hiss, the grenade landed at his feet. A suffocating cloud of acrid fog billowed out, obscuring his vision. "Stay low and follow my voice," he whispered urgently.

Hearing the footsteps of their pursuers closing in, he looked for an escape route through the cloying smoke. Catching a flash of movement out of the corner of his eye, he turned to see the blurry form of the helicopter pilot charging Eden.

Rushing to help her, he saw the pilot wrest Eden's gun from her hand, his fist connecting with her head and sending her crumpling to the floor. Then the pair were swallowed up by a cloud of drifting smoke.

Desperately searching for Abbie through the blinding haze, Ethan's blood ran cold when he heard her terrified scream. Frantic to reach her, he stormed forward blindly. Suddenly, Edgar appeared from out of nowhere, lunging at him. Before Ethan could aim his gun, the mobster's fist cracked across his head, sending him staggering backward.

Taking advantage of his disoriented state, Edgar grabbed his arm and pried his gun from his hand. Desperate to regain control of the weapon, Ethan struck out blindly. His fist slammed into Edgar's jaw, sending the mobster reeling. But before he could land a second punch, the pilot joined the fight, landing a brutal blow to his temple. As blinding pain exploded in his head, he was racked with anguish at the thought he might fail Abbie.

Outnumbered now, he fought back wildly as the need to subdue his attackers and rescue her pulsed through him with every ragged breath. For a moment it seemed as though he was wearing the men down, but then the tide turned against him. Edgar slammed his fist into Ethan's jaw, sending a kaleidoscope of jumbled colors swimming in his vision. Capitalizing on his momentary weakness, the pilot directed a powerful kick to the back of his knees that buckled his legs and sent him crashing to the ground, following the blow with a vicious punch to his head.

Stunned, he blacked out for a second. When he opened

his eyes, the smoke had cleared. Edgar was dragging Abbie to the helicopter as she kicked and struggled.

Ethan fought to his way to his feet, but Edgar was already forcing Abbie into the chopper. As the pilot lifted the craft off the landing pad, Ethan saw Edgar in the rear of the helicopter, his gun trained on Abbie.

With fear-fueled adrenaline pumping through his veins, Ethan raced toward the chopper. Launching himself in the air, he vaulted onto the craft's landing skid. Muscles screaming in protest as he fought against the powerful pull of the wind from the rotor blades, he pulled himself up into the cockpit.

Distracted by Ethan's sudden appearance, Edgar turned his attention away from Abbie. Seizing the moment, Abbie elbowed him in the ribs and grabbed his wrist. Twisting the gun from his hands, she took control of the weapon.

Assured of her safety, Ethan focused on overtaking the pilot. As they battled for the control of the helicopter's cyclic stick, the aircraft lurched dangerously.

Striking the pilot in the face, he took control of the helicopter. He was bringing the craft back down when he caught the glint of steel out of the corner of his eye. The pilot had pulled a knife and was lunging for him.

Ethan ducked to avoid the blade. Grabbing the man's wrist, he twisted it until his opponent was forced to release his hold on the weapon.

"Ethan! Look out!" Abbie shouted as the knife clattered to the floor.

Her terrified scream snapped his attention back to their trajectory. A short distance ahead, an imposing cliff loomed directly in their path.

With a final punch, Ethan knocked the pilot out. Grabbing the cyclic, he shoved it upward, holding his breath as the chopper lurched and then climbed steeply into the sky, just missing the cliff face. Heart pounding, he steadied the craft and brought it back down to the landing pad. As he powered it off, he saw blue lights flashing in the distance, accompanied by the blare of sirens.

Turning to Abbie, Ethan helped her disembark. Wrapping her arms around him, she hugged him so tightly he could barely breathe. "I'm so glad you're okay," he told her, his voice breaking as he gently wiped away the tears of relief streaming down her face.

"I have you to thank for that. Again." She rolled her eyes teasingly. "We have to stop making a habit of this."

Eden raced up to meet them. Opening the door to the copilot's side of the chopper, she aimed her weapon at the pilot, who was just regaining consciousness. "Step out slowly with your hands in the air," she ordered the man as the sheriff and his deputies swarmed around the chopper.

"I called an ambulance for Mark and the Sheriff's Department for backup," Eden hurriedly explained. "Is everyone all right?"

"We are, thanks to you," Ethan affirmed with a grateful smile. "Are you okay?"

"I'm fine." Her mouth quirked upward. "I'm going to have an impressive shiner, though. If you're set here, I'm going to go and meet the ambulance team. A couple of deputies are waiting to accompany the paramedics when they tend to Mark. I told them there's a K-9 guarding the perp and suggested they wait for me to go in with them. As soon as they're all set, I'll bring Zane to you."

Ethan shot her a grateful smile. "Great. Oh, and would

you let the deputies know Mark has Vince and Winona locked up on the boat that's moored at the dock?"

"Sure thing." She nodded, pausing for a moment before continuing. "I realize the Romola family is on the hook for kidnapping Abbie now. But they're powerful and connected. If Mark isn't willing to testify against them, do you still have enough to dismantle their organization?"

Ethan bobbed his head in affirmation. "If Mark doesn't roll over on them, my hunch is the information on the flash drive will be enough to bring them down. And there's a slim chance Winona might also agree to play ball and share what she knows."

Smiling triumphantly, Abbie whipped out her phone and waved it in the air. "Will their confessions do? I recorded everything."

Ethan had never been as proud of Abbie as he was in that moment. He'd seen her overcome terrible adversity and display incredible courage, but her quick thinking and bravery while fighting for her life amazed him. "That will most definitely do! You're incredible!" He beamed, lifting her up in his arms and twirling her around. "Great work!"

Eden pumped her fists in the air. "Yeah! Just so you know, I'm going to recruit Abbie to come and work for me as a private investigator, Ethan," she warned him with a smile.

He shot Eden a mock glare, one eyebrow arching upward. "I found her first," he warned teasingly. "And didn't you say something about going to get my K-9?"

Chuckling, Eden saluted. "Yes, sir!"

A few minutes later, Eden returned with Zane. Then she headed off to give her statement to the deputies.

Abbie chuckled as the K-9 greeted her with an enthusiastic lick. Watching the deputies Eden had summoned load the handcuffed Edgar, Vince, Winona, Mark and the pilot into their van, peace settled over her. It was over. It was really over!

"I'm so proud of you! You were brilliant," Ethan praised. "Leaving your camera for me to find with the photo of the chalet cued up on the display screen was quick thinking. I never would have located you in time otherwise. And you were amazing going up against Edgar in the helicopter. You saw your chance and you didn't hesitate to grab it."

"When I saw Vince shoot you, I was so afraid," she blurted. "But I knew if you were okay you'd find my camera and get my message."

"The bullet just grazed me. When I went down from the impact, I hit my head on a rock and I blacked out. When I came to, the Romolas were taking you away on their boat. You're safe now. They'll be going to prison for a very long time."

Their conversation was cut short when one of the sheriff's deputies approached them.

"Sorry to interrupt you," the man apologized, "but if you're feeling up to it, we need to get your statements. And, sir, you should have the EMTs look at your shoulder."

Ethan waved off the man's suggestion. "It's nothing. I patched it up."

Abbie pinned him with her best you're-not-worming-your-way-out-of-this look. "You were struck by a bullet and knocked unconscious. You need to let them check you out."

Ethan opened his mouth to argue, but she held up her hand. Recognizing the futility of arguing the point, he surrendered. “Okay. I’ll go see them while you talk to the deputies.”

As soon as Abbie had finished giving her account of the incident, she went looking for Ethan. Scanning the law enforcement officers congregated at the scene, dread congealed in her veins when she didn’t see him in the crowd. Had he left without saying goodbye?

Spotting Eden, she hurried to the woman. “Have you seen Ethan?” she blurted.

“Abbie! I was just coming to find you. Ethan’s fine, but the EMTs talked him into getting his shoulder wound stitched up at the hospital. He has a slight concussion, so they thought it would be best if he stayed there overnight for observation. Ethan asked me if I minded bringing you home with me until he’s released. He doesn’t want you to be alone until we’re sure the Romolas aren’t going to somehow manage to get the opportunity to post bail.”

“Is that really necessary? The Romolas are in custody. It’s over now, isn’t it?”

“Yes, but until we’re sure they don’t make bail, Ethan’s right to play it safe.”

Abbie’s heart stuttered at the thought that, even behind bars, the Romolas could still be a threat. She’d do well to remember that the danger was still very real. If the Romolas made bail, they’d come for her.

Taking a deep breath, she lifted her chin. Fiery resolve sparked in her eyes. If they did, she’d be waiting for them. She was prepared to do whatever she had to do to ensure they could never hurt her or anyone else ever again.

FOURTEEN

Ethan woke the next morning to the chiming of his cell phone. Glancing at the screen, he saw Hunter's name. He'd hoped it might be Abbie phoning, but most likely she was still sleeping after the ordeal she'd endured.

With a sigh, he answered the call, trying to keep his disappointment from his voice. He knew Abbie was in the best of hands with Eden, but that didn't stop him from worrying about her. "Hi, Hunter."

"I have news!" she enthused brightly. "First, how are you and Abbie? Eden called and filled me in on what happened. Scary stuff."

"We're fine, thanks in no small part to you, Jaret and Eden."

"I'm glad. And congratulations on dismantling the Romolas' criminal empire. Great work!"

"It was a team effort. And I'm grateful you were part of that team. So, what's the good news?"

"Brock was able to decrypt the flash drive Vito left for Abbie. It contains files with information that proves, beyond a shadow of a doubt, that the Romolas are key players in the Northeast drug trade. Everything is detailed! Drug shipments. Financial records proving they were funneling money into offshore accounts after laundering it thorough shell companies. Proof that Edgar ordered hits and that his organization was also carrying out hits for hire. There's a list of targets. Abbie was on that list. And Landon wasn't the victim of a random burglary. His name was on the list of hits the Romolas were paid to carry-out. Coupled with the confessions Abbie captured, Edgar, Vince, Gabriella—Winona, I mean—and their associates are going to be behind bars for the next several decades."

"That's going to make a lot of people very happy."

"For sure," Hunter agreed. "Speaking of your ex-partner, Eden told me about Gabriella staging her death and undergoing a twisted metamorphosis in an attempt to join Edgar. I can only imagine how you must feel."

"Foolish pretty much covers it. I had no idea she was capable of that level of treachery."

"You must be relieved it's over."

"I wish I could say with a hundred percent certainty this case is a wrap. We're proceeding with caution for the next few days until we're certain the Romolas can't wriggle their way out of custody. If they do, there's a very good chance they'll try and finish what they started. Eden invited Abbie to stay with her through the weekend, just so we can be sure the Romolas don't post bail."

"That's wise. The silver lining to all of this is you got to reconnect with Abbie. Since she's here through the summer, you'll get to see her often."

Uncertain of how to respond, Ethan hesitated, letting silence hang between them.

"Ethan?" Hunter prompted, breaking the uncomfortable pause.

Ethan swallowed back the lump of emotion rising in

his throat. "Abbie is ready to go back to building her new life. Once I know for certain that the Romola family is no longer a threat to her, it will be time for me to go back to mine. She won't need me anymore."

"Did she tell you that? More importantly, did you tell her how you feel about her? It's obvious you care deeply for her."

Ethan fell silent again.

"Oh, Ethan," Hunter sighed. "You are so stubborn. Can't you see she wants *you* to be a part of that life? Even in the short amount of time I spent with you both, it's clear as day you two are meant to be together. You know, I had a chance to talk with her while she was at the lighthouse, and she shared a bit about her childhood with me. She had it rough. She grew up in foster homes and never had any real family ties. She doesn't give her heart easily, because everyone she's ever offered it to has thrown it back in her face.

"If you don't want to break her heart, keep in mind that you're the person with the greatest potential to hurt her. You walked away from her once. She's afraid you'll leave her again. She also thinks you find her repulsive because of her scars."

"I couldn't care less about her scars, aside from wishing I could have prevented Vito from hurting her. If I could go back and try to extract a different outcome, I would, but in my eyes, she's perfect."

"My advice, then? If you want her in her life—and you're crazy if you don't—stop being so hardheaded and tell her how you feel."

Propelling her kayak across the glassy surface of the lake, Abbie tried to quiet her tumultuous thoughts. Slicing her oar through the water, she surrendered to the soothing rhythm of her paddle strokes and let herself drift in the tranquil embrace of this wilderness paradise. But the serenity surrounding her was a cruel contrast to the tempest of uncertainty raging inside her.

"It's so peaceful out here, isn't it?" Eden asked, drawing her from her ruminations.

Gripping her paddle a little too tightly, Abbie nodded, feigning a lightheartedness she didn't feel. Ethan had told Hunter he'd join them as soon as he was discharged today. When she'd called the hospital to check on him before heading out to kayak with Eden, she'd been told he'd been released at eight. Yet he hadn't called. Hadn't texted. And he hadn't shown up.

"Thanks for suggesting we do this." Abbie's lips curved upward, but she knew her smile didn't make it to her eyes. Her joy was clouded by her fear that Ethan was distancing himself from her again, like he had in New York.

"You'll get some great photos today." Eden grinned. "The way the sky is reflected in the lake will make for a beautiful backdrop."

"The clouds look like giant cotton balls."

"Look. Up ahead," Eden whispered softly.

Bringing her kayak to a stop alongside Eden's, she sucked in an awestruck breath. A mother loon, looking regal with her glossy black head and white neckband, was gliding across the lake. Her two chicks were riding piggyback, brown fluff balls of down nestled cozily on her black-and-white feathers.

Grabbing her camera, Abbie captured an entire series of shots of the beautiful family before the mother loon headed for the lush greenery at the edge of the lake and she and her chicks disappeared from sight.

"That was amazing," she told Eden as they paddled back to the house. "The loons were absolutely gorgeous."

Eden nodded toward the shoreline. "Speaking of gorgeous, you have a visitor."

Glancing up, Abbie's heart seized at the sight of Ethan standing at the edge of the lake. She'd missed him so much in the short time they'd been apart. She couldn't paddle to the shore fast enough.

"Hi, Ethan," Eden greeted him as he helped them drag their kayaks out of the water. "I'm guessing you want to talk to Abbie. When you guys are ready, come back to the house. I'll have iced tea and pastries waiting for you," she told them as she strolled off.

"I missed you," Abbie blurted. Straight away, she regretted the telling slipup. She didn't want to do anything to jeopardize this chance to build a relationship. If she revealed the depth of her feelings for him too soon, she'd scare him away. But how on earth was she going to be able to hold back the tidal wave of emotion threatening to burst through her chest? She deflected to the first neutral thought that came to mind. "How are you feeling?"

"Great, other than wrestling with a serious case of nerves."

"Nerves? After you just took down a crime family practically single-handedly? You can handle anything."

His eyes flicked to hers. Seeing the turmoil swirling in their depths, her pulse stuttered.

Ethan rubbed the back of his neck. "There's something I need to tell you." He paused, his eyes zeroing in on hers again, but holding her gaze this time.

Her heart plummeted like a free-falling elevator. *He's leaving.* The much-yearned-for relationship with him she thought she was going to have a chance to build was about to crash and burn before it even started. She should probably be grateful he wasn't walking out of her life without voicing his intent, but the polite gesture didn't make the realization she was about to lose him again hurt any less. "Just say it," she rasped out, her heart aching.

He raked a hand through his hair. "I'm sorry. I get that you'd like us to be friends, but I can't offer you that."

Abbie simply stared. His words were salt in a gaping wound in her heart. She was saved from replying when he pressed on.

"Friendship isn't enough for me. I want more," he affirmed. Reaching for her hand, he entwined his fingers with hers before continuing. "You need to know that when we were in the tunnel at the chalet, after I kissed you, I wanted to tell you how much you mean to me. I couldn't work up the nerve to share what was in my heart, because I was scared of my feelings for you—scared of letting you close."

"But why?" she stammered.

"I was engaged once, and it ended badly. I thought Sondra loved me, but she left me for someone else. After that, I walled off my heart. I was determined to never to put myself in a position of vulnerability like that again. I refused to let anyone get close. Then I met you, and you bulldozed past my defenses, despite my best efforts to keep you at arm's length.

"I realize, now, I've been stubborn and thickheaded, refusing to see what was right in front of me. I love you, Abbie Renforth. And if you think I'm telling you this out of some sort of misplaced remorse for what I wasn't able to stop Vito from doing to you, you're sorely mistaken. Your scars only enhance your beauty. They're a testament to your strength and your courage. I'm sorry I've wasted so much time hiding from the truth and running from my feelings for you. I'm sorry I left you then, but I promise I'll never do it again. I'm done running. I'm not scared anymore."

Swallowing hard, she blinked back the tears threatening to flow, not daring to believe what she was hearing. "I survived after the job I loved was stripped away from me. I survived after my life was nearly ended by a crazed serial killer. I survived after you walked away from me in New York. I know for certain there's one thing I can't survive, and that's losing you if you walk away again. I love you Ethan!"

Ethan's hold on her hand tightened gently. "I promise I'm not going anywhere. I want to spend time with you when we *aren't* going head to head with a mafia family. I want to get to know every facet of the amazing woman you are. I know you're going to be busy with the artist-in-residency program for the next few months, but can I see you when you have downtime?"

Her heart rejoicing, and her face stretched by a smile so wide it hurt, Abbie bobbed her head in eager assent. "There's nothing I'd like more."

The last time Ethan had saved her, he'd left without warning, exiting her life after the tempest had passed. But this time? This time he was going to stay.

EPILOGUE

Four months later...

"Abbs!" Ethan called. "Wait up!"

Sprinting ahead of him as they trekked a tranquil woodland path, alight in breathtakingly vibrant hues of crimson, orange and gold on this sunny October day, Abbie, his own bright ray of sunshine, hurried toward the moose that frequented the lake at the end of the trail, eager to photograph them. At her side, Zane loped happily. His German shepherd was as besotted with her as he was.

Peaceful interludes like this one were such a blessing. So was sharing them with Abbie. In the past four months, they'd gone on countless dates, making the most of all this serene wilderness backcountry had to offer. Every adventure they shared in the great outdoors drew him closer to the woman he loved more with each passing day.

The Romola family had been brought to justice. Abbie's leg was almost fully healed now, a slight hitch in her stride the only hint of the ordeal she'd endured at the hands of the Spitting Image Slayer. The summer in the artist-in-residency program had helped her recover from the physical and emotional trauma she'd gone through. Her work reflected her newfound peace and happiness, and her freelance photography career was skyrocketing.

There would be time for her to take more photos soon. Right now, he had something he was eager to show her. He couldn't wait another second.

Catching up with her, he took her hand, drawing her to his side. His heart was pounding so hard he was certain it would explode. This was it. It was all-or-nothing time. He prayed it wouldn't be the latter.

Dropping down to one knee in front of her, Ethan pulled a ring from his pocket. Sunlight gleamed off the oval-cut diamond set in the center of a twisted gold band as he held it out to her. Her mouth dropped open, shocked disbelief flashing across her beautiful face.

With his love for her shining in his eyes, he shared his heart. "Abbie Renforth, I want to spend the rest of my life with you. I believe the Lord made us to be together. Will you do me the honor of being my wife? Please tell me your answer is yes."

"Oh, Ethan. Yes! Most emphatically yes!" she cried out, tears of joy spilling down her cheeks. "You're my hero, and my soul mate. When I was in danger, you rescued me. You helped me heal physically and spiritually. When I turned my back on God, blaming Him for what happened to me, you steered me back to His loving arms. You offered me support and encouragement, and you prayed with me. No one else in my entire life has ever shown me that kind of compassion. That profound a depth of love. I love you with all my heart and soul. There's no one I'd rather share my life with."

Humbled by the ardor underscoring her words, Ethan didn't dare speak. Instead, he gathered her into his arms. Hugging her tight, he let his lips do the talking, pouring all of his love for her into a kiss that sealed his promise.

* * * * *

Dear Reader,

The book you're holding is my first Harlequin novel, and proof that dreams come true. Thanks so much for sharing this milestone with me!

When I began plotting Abbie and Ethan's story, I knew Abbie's character would possess remarkable strength and courage given the ordeal she survived. Abbie doesn't need rescuing—she needs someone who sees her as whole despite her scars. Ethan is that someone, but he clings to the misplaced certainty he failed her in the past and fears he might fail her again.

As Ethan and Abbie battle side by side against a merciless mob family, they find strength in each other and a love that refuses to surrender. I hope you enjoyed their victory.

Until the next adventure,
Lisa